Surrogate for the Sheikh

A Novel By

Annabelle Winters

BOOKS BY ANNABELLE WINTERS

THE CURVES FOR SHEIKHS SERIES
Curves for the Sheikh
Flames for the Sheikh
Hostage for the Sheikh
Single for the Sheikh
Stockings for the Sheikh
Untouched for the Sheikh
Surrogate for the Sheikh
Stars for the Sheikh
Shelter for the Sheikh

Surrogate for the Sheikh

A NOVEL BY

Annabelle Winters

2017
Rainshine Books
USA

Copyright Notice

Copyright © 2017 by Annabelle Winters
All Rights Reserved by Author
www.annabellewinters.com
ab@annabellewinters.com

If you'd like to copy, reproduce, sell, or distribute any part of this text, please obtain the explicit, written permission of the author first. Note that you should feel free to tell your spouse, lovers, friends, and coworkers how happy this book made you. Have a wonderful evening!

Cover Design by S. Lee

ISBN: 978-1543008227

0 1 2 3 4 5 6 7 8 9

Surrogate for the Sheikh

1

"Did you know you're eight times more likely to wear red when you're ovulating?"

Gracie Garner turned bright red as she frowned up at Jean Baylor, the much taller (and thinner . . .) soccer coach from St. Louis who was now on her way to becoming a soccer mom, last Gracie had heard. Jean had married the barrel-shaped security guard of a Middle-Eastern Sheikh (Nasser), and since it turned out that security guards to billionaire kings were themselves millionaires, was now retired and living with her gigantic Arab husband in a gigantic house near Lake Tahoe.

"You're visiting Oklahoma? Sweet!" Gracie had said when Jean called to invite her to a shareholder's banquet that some rich Arabs were hosting in Tulsa and for which her husband's new U.S.-based personal security company had been hired. "And you're sure I can come to this banquet even though I'm not a shareholder of anything besides my niece's lemonade stand? Which is starting up later this summer, by the way. I can get you a discount. Maybe even some extra sugar cubes on the back end."

"Oh, I can give out as many invitations as I want," Jean had said over the phone, totally ignoring the awesome quip about the lemonade stand. "After heading up Sheikh Nasser's security for so many years, my husband is almost royalty himself. In fact he was the one who asked if I had any friends from Tulsa that I wanted to invite! So I told him to get you two passes and to seat you at our table. It's no problem. I want to see you, Grace Garner! It's been how long . . . almost ten years, I think! God, are we that—"

"Two passes?" Gracie had said, gulping at the reminder that she was single again and Jean Baylor—the awkward, shy, flat-chested girl whose clothes never seemed to fit right—was now married to a millionaire who was "almost royalty." The world seriously belonged to skinny women, it seemed—not full-figured, thirty-something middle-school teachers whose old clothes didn't even fit, let alone fit right!

Surrogate for the Sheikh

"Of course two passes, Gracie. I take care of my old friends. And it's a black tie event, so tell that man of yours to clean himself up and rent a tux and—"

"There's no man, Jean," Gracie had said quietly as she looked down and touched her belly unconsciously. "Jonathan and I . . . well, I'll explain when I see you, yeah?"

"Oh, wow, really? Oh, I'm sorry, Grace. I'm just going by what I saw on Facebook a couple of months ago. There were all those cute pictures of you with . . . anyway. Whatever. I'm sorry. I didn't—" Jean had started to say before Gracie stopped her.

"No, it's a good thing," Gracie had said hurriedly, perhaps trying to convince herself of it more than anything. After all, she had ended it and so by definition it was a good thing. Leaving Jonathan was a good thing. Yes, Gracie, it was good and right, smart and sensible. Sensible to leave a man whose love for you bordered on worship, who made more in a month than you make in a year, who would've given you a ring, a house, an SUV, a country-club membership . . . everything but the one thing you want: a baby bump. "We weren't a good fit, and neither of us are getting any younger, and so I told him we should just—"

"Wait, *you* broke up with *him*?" Jean had asked, her voice rising to that nasally pitch that reminded Gracie of why they hadn't kept in close contact even after playing soccer together all the way through high school back in St. Louis. "Grace, why? Oh, God, I can't wait to see you. Listen, I'll have the passes—"

Gracie had swallowed her pride and gulped down her anger, frowning into the phone as she stopped a wonderfully caustic retort from making its way past her pursed lips. She had smiled as she listened to Jean go on about how she'd have the passes delivered by "private courier" or something, perhaps in a stagecoach with rabbit-footmen and moon-faced gnomes at the reins.

Um, you married a security guard, she wanted to snap at Jean. And "almost royalty" isn't royalty, honey. The word "almost" is the clue. It means nope, not quite there. Sorry. Maybe in your next life you'll be a queen, you skinny, annoying bi—

But of course Gracie held her tongue. Nothing wrong with marrying a bear-sized security guard with ten million in the bank, she had reminded herself as she calmed down to the point where she was almost embarrassed by her own thoughts. Wow, I can be a bitch, can't I—at least in my thoughts if not my words, she told herself as Jean finally wound up her Marie-Antoinette speech about how she could hand out passes to the street-urchins from the south side of Tulsa if she wanted, because she was *so* awesome and her husband was *so* close to being royalty. Lah-dee-dah!

So Gracie let Jean send the two passes anyway, even though it was going to be Gracie flying solo, like it

Surrogate for the Sheikh

was most nights now, after "the conversation" with Jonathan—the conversation that Jonathan himself had started when he said he wasn't going to wear condoms anymore because he had gotten "snipped."

"Sorry, what?" Gracie had said as she stared across the Formica-covered diner table at Jonathan's long, pale face as he sipped his strawberry shake and glanced up at her. "You did what?"

He had burped and leaned back against the shiny blue rexine of the booth. "A vasectomy. This way there's no argument about kids and all that. We're set. Like we talked about."

Gracie had felt the blood rise and fall so fast she almost fainted into her pancakes, blinking as she stared at the maple syrup and wondered if that side of bacon was talking to her. After all, that would have made more sense than what Jonathan was saying as he gurgled down the strawberry shake which looked way too pink to be strawberry. Pepto Bismol, perhaps.

"Talked about it when?" she said when she finally caught up and realized she wasn't face-first in the pancakes and so she could finish them after Jonathan smiled and said he was joking, thereby proving what she had always known about him but had chosen to overlook: that the man had no sense of humor—never laughed at a joke, couldn't tell if someone was joking, and clearly couldn't tell a joke himself without creating alarm, indignation, and disgust.

"That night when we had the abortion discussion,"

Jonathan had said. "Remember? Oh, wait. You probably don't remember, because you threw a fit and walked away after I got to the part where I said I was sick of using condoms and if you weren't going to get on the pill then we'd have to agree that if you got pregnant, you'd have an abortion."

"I remember that part," Gracie had said slowly, her jaw going tight, big brown eyes narrowing to dark slits as if she already knew where this conversation was going to end up—where she was going to *take* this conversation, whether parsnip-faced Jonathan was expecting it or not. It was almost a relief, in a sick, twisted way. Like she suddenly had an excuse to . . . oh, God, had she been waiting for an excuse?

But speaking of twisted, she had thought as she poked her pancakes and wondered if she should eat before or after she dumped his ass. Was he doing the same? Was he trying to get her to break up with him?

She had studied his long white face, those light blue eyes that had once seemed so charming but now looked a bit too close together. "Yeah, I remember that part," she said again, finally deciding to hold off on the pancakes. "The part where you wanted me to choose between jacking myself up with anti-pregnancy hormones or agree to some future surgery just because you're sick of wearing condoms."

"Grace, every goddamn chick in America is on the pill starting at age thirteen! That was the whole point of the sexual revolution!" he had said, nonchalantly stirring the foam at the bottom of his shake as he snorted and shook.

"Actually the pill was just one of the many enablers of the sexual revolution," Gracie had snapped. "And since you bring it up, the actual point of the sexual revolution was that a woman owns her own damn body, which means she chooses whether to have sex, whether to take the pill, and most certainly whether or not to terminate a pregnancy." She had frowned for a moment, prying her sausage links out from beneath the pancakes before taking a breath and glancing up from her plate, lowering her voice as she spoke. "And this is the first I'm hearing about how much you hate condoms." A pause and another breath. "Is this about our recent . . . um . . . *challenges* in the bedroom?"

Jonathan had turned pinker than his Pepto-Bismol shake as his jaw went slack for a moment before he narrowed those blue eyes and stared at her, accusation in one eye, hurt in the other, self-consciousness all over that long, pale horse-face. He snorted now, leaning back and then forward like he was on a rexine rocking chair. "I *knew* you were going to make it about that. Sexual performance isn't up to just one person, you know. Maybe if you weren't so cold and disinterested, it'd be easier for me to get it . . . get it going."

"Whoa," said Gracie, frowning and raising her hands and showing him the timeout signal, which seemed to confuse him since he never watched sports and was never around kids and clearly had been such a good kid that he had never been put in a timeout situation by mommy dearest. "Stop, Jonathan. Just stop, OK?" she had said quickly, wondering why she felt this strange contempt rise up in her as she looked at this man like he was a stranger suddenly, a person who repulsed her now, the change happening so quickly that she couldn't understand it. "I've never blamed you for a moment about . . . about that. In fact *I'm* the one who always says that sex is about *two* people, and sometimes one person just isn't aroused for whatever reason. And that's OK! Hell, women fake it all the time!" She paused and pretended to burp so she could hide her smile. "It's really not a big deal. You don't need to feel all the pressure to perform. I told you that if it's something we need to work on together, I'm all for it." She gulped as she said that last line, blinking and breaking eye contact as she wondered again where that sudden feeling of repulsion was coming from, why she suddenly didn't want to work on *anything* with Jonathan, that she was done and now she couldn't wait to finish her pancakes and sausage and head home all alone, feeling full and satisfied, happy and free! What. The. Hell.

Jonathan's smile had gotten so tight that his lips were white as ash. Gracie had seen that look before—it happened every time he freaked out about not staying hard when they were having sex. She didn't care nearly as much as he did—hell, of course there were times she wasn't aroused and she just moaned and groaned her way through it anyway. It sucked that a man couldn't hide it or fake it like a woman—but hey, that was life. Deal with it like a man, for God's sake, she had wanted to say across that table. Have the balls to deal with your limp cock, came the wisecrack in her mind, but she faked another burp and then immediately started eating, digging into those pancakes and slicing that sausage, poking at the overeasy eggs and reaching across the table for the salt and pepper shakers.

Jonathan's smile seemed to get tighter, his eyes seeming to lose their color as his face went red. Soon everything about him was red except those eyeballs, and Gracie just chewed and stared at him like he was an alien lizard minion who had landed in the diner and wanted control over her body.

It was cold and cruel, but hell, Gracie wasn't going to deal with a man who gave her a choice like that. Did he even *bother* to look up what the pill does to a woman's body? Yes, it could actually be a good thing for women with endometriosis and some other complications, but mostly women just dealt with the side effects because of the obvious benefits.

And it wasn't like she was just being a bitch by not going back on the pill. She'd tried several different brands over the years, and they all gave her terrible acne and swelling. She wasn't going to waddle around with a face like a pin-cushion, ankles the size of a child's thighs, and a belly like a gas-balloon just so thin-lipped Jonathan could wake up his sleeping lizard. And the alternative? Agree to have an abortion if she got pregnant? Seriously? Should she just hand over custody of her goddamn *womb* to him? Hell no, Jonathan, she had said. I'm not the kind of woman who's going to simply . . . . simply *obey*!

Of course, she had said she wasn't that kind of woman, but a part of her whispered along that Jonathan wasn't that kind of man . . . the kind of man Gracie would want to obey, the kind of man who could *make* this strict Oklahoma schoolteacher want to obey. God, men were such wimps these days!

She touched her neck as she frowned at those pancakes, telling herself to stop eating and talk to this man who seemed close to having a stroke across from her. After all, his presumptuousness aside, he had gone ahead and done something drastic to *his* body after she refused to do anything to hers! Wasn't that something? Wasn't that love? Or was it just lame?!

Or maybe it's the ultimate act of presumptuousness and ownership over my body, she had thought as she speared a sausage link with her fork and took a bite. Like because he has the cock he can just decide that if we stay together, we're never having kids? Well, it's my *womb*, honeybug. I get to decide.

Now she smiled, thinking for a moment that God, in a way she was almost *relieved* that as badly as she felt the need to someday be a mother, it wouldn't be this wimp's kids she'd be popping out! Oh, *God*, she was such a bitch in the privacy of her mind! If anyone knew . . .

"New dress?" came Jean's voice through the privacy of that sausage-shaped daydream. "You know you're eight times more likely to wear red when you're ovulating."

"Huh? What?" said Gracie, blinking as she felt the self-consciousness kick in. Now she remembered she was in that hotel ballroom, single and unaccompanied, and she suddenly felt almost naked in that knee-length red dress, no stockings or hose, not even Spanx to keep her tight. She had arrived way too early and had been standing alone with a glass of champagne, lost in that daydream, a part of her still in that daydream.

"Jean! Hi! Wow, you look . . ." Gracie began to say even as she thought it had been a mistake to come, that how the hell was she going to make small talk with Jean when they hadn't even been particularly good friends at the best of times.

Oh, Lord, someone save me, she thought as she tried to figure out how to respond to the vaguely unsettling—and certainly inappropriate—comment about ovulation. Yeah, it might have come across fine if Jean had a sense of humor, but the woman was in the same category as Jonathan as far as that went. Ovulation jokes? Really? Oh, Lord, please save me before I have to deliver a comeback to an *ovulation* joke! Help!

Gracie took a breath and tried to craft a sentence that wasn't too bitchy or cold, but then from the shadows he came, arriving silent like the breeze, just the sound of his voice enough to make her turn.

"Ladies, relax. Sheikh Dhomaar is here!" came the booming voice, the sound thundering down from above, like it really was a god announcing his arrival "I heard that a woman is ovulating in this part of the room, and so I arrived immediately!" The voice was deep and resonant, cocky and confident, smoothly accented, perfectly pitched, the delivery coming with a lazy energy that made Gracie feel a spontaneous tingle beneath her red dress as she blinked and turned.

She had to look up to see his face, and even then she had to blink away the mist that had enveloped her in that daydream, disorienting her as those thoughts of Jonathan and limp sausage links, salt-shakers and vasectomies, baby bumps and bloating all swirled around and disappeared into the ether, leaving just this thirty-something unmarried schoolteacher standing on a thick carpet in the elegant Grand Ballroom of the Rega Royal hotel in downtown Tulsa, red dress with black panties beneath, bra tight around her heavy bosom, soft boobs feeling surprisingly firm, big bottom feeling unusually secure and strangely tingly, like everyone and everything was telling Gracie she was . . . she was . . . she was . . . ovulating?!

She blinked through that mist and took a quick breath, taking in the sight of this handsome Arabian man who was fully focused on her now, facing her front and center, tailored tuxedo that looked like it hadn't been made by human hands, the black of the cloth so rich it almost made her swoon, the shirt so impeccably white, the strong cut of the cotton broadcloth leading her eyes up along the ridge of his neckline to his thick, muscular neck, large Adam's apple, strong jawline set in a half-smile, cheekbones like high desert cliffs, the ridges straight and symmetrical, catching the soft overhead light and casting his brown skin in smooth shadow, making his dark stubble glisten like black diamonds. And those lips. Oh, God, so full and thick. Dark red and luscious.

Then she looked up.

She looked up into his eyes.

2

His eyes broke through that mist, cast off that spell, pulling her into a new spell so quick she had to shift on her feet and spread her legs a bit so she could be sure she wouldn't stumble where she stood in her red dress, entranced by those green eyes. Green eyes set like dark emeralds above his high cheekbones, sharp greens staring into her baby browns.

"I heard that a woman is ovulating in this part of the room and so I arrived immediately," he said with that cocky grin which somehow made the comment *completely* appropriate for a black tie banquet at the Rega Royal's Grand Ballroom.

"Wow," she said without stopping to think. "Your hearing must be very good if you can hear a woman ovulate. What does it sound like?"

"It sounds like . . . this," he said with no hesitation as he leaned close, doing it slowly and deliberately, his cheek almost touching hers as he blew gently into the brown curls of her hair along her temples. His fingertips grazed her side as he withdrew, nothing but the thin red satin of her dress separating his hand from her hips, his skin from hers, the touch so shocking that she gasped and drew back from him, breaking eye contact as she touched her hair and blinked and gasped again.

"So it sounds like sexual harassment?" she said firmly, looking up at him as she tried to control herself even though everything inside her was going certifiably nuts, with tingles and tremors, bursts of electricity, splashes of light, like it was a Fourth of July rehearsal under that red dress, inside those black pan—

He grinned as he looked down at her, his handsome face not showing the slightest flinch, his eye contact strong and merciless. "Should I call security?" he asked through that grin. "Or would you rather just scream?"

"OK, so now you've moved from sexual harassment to straight up sexism," Gracie said, folding her arms under her boobs and tapping one foot unconsciously as she felt an annoyingly playful smile break on her round face. "I would do *neither*. I'd just *jab* you in the eyeballs and *kick* you in the crotch. I teach my kids that they should never have to rely on someone else to defend them, and I walk the talk, buddy."

"How many kids?" he said, effortlessly diverting the conversation. Now his smile tightened, green eyes narrowed, and he shamelessly glanced down her curves, taking in the swell of her breasts, the contours of her wide hips, her thick bare calves all tight and smooth in those black heels. He glanced at her ring finger, blinked once, and then coolly looked into her eyes like he couldn't give a damn what she thought about where his eyes—and perhaps his mind—had just been. "And how old?"

"Eighteen," she said, rolling her tongue inside her mouth as she held her posture, that first blast of arousal now settling into a steady buzz that she could feel everywhere under that red dress, behind that tight bra, under those black satin panties which seemed to be riding up into her bottom a little.

"Eighteen years old? You must have been a very young mother," he said, frowning and glancing at her ring finger again.

"No," she said. "Eighteen kids. I've got eighteen kids."

The man's eyebrows rose and he cocked his head to the side like he actually believed her. A quick glance at her round belly and then he looked back into her eyes and cocked his head to the other side. A last glance at her ringless fingers, and finally he smiled and snapped his fingers. "Ah, I know. You are an egg donor. Perhaps also a surrogate for women who are unable to carry a child. Yes?"

Gracie half frowned half smiled as she looked up at this tall, handsome foreigner who really seemed to believe that she had eighteen kids, and had already decided that he had figured out how and why. It wasn't a bad guess, she had to admit. No ring on her finger. And eighteen is way too many for a straight-up surrogate her age, so egg donor plus surrogate was a smart guess. Most importantly though, how old did he think she was, she wondered as she touched her hair again and firmed up her buttocks and smiled up at him.

"Yeah, you know they don't pay us teachers jack in this country," she said with a shrug. "So I just harvest my eggs and rent out my womb for cash. That's a great guess, by the way. Not sexist at all."

"*How* is that sexist?" he cried, throwing his long, thick arms up in mock exasperation, ridges of his chest muscles showing through the fitted white shirt beneath his tuxedo jacket. He kept those mammoth arms up, his wing-span on full display as he took a full circle in front of Gracie before stopping to face her and grinning wide. "*You* are the one who says you are mother to eighteen children, and I am the sexist one? I cannot win with you, yes? Ya Allah, this country and its women! I love it! Who are you? Tell me your name! You must join our table so I can have some entertaining conversations tonight! Perfect! I was just dreading having to converse with these old Arabs and their quiet wives, but now things are looking up. Come. To my table with your eggs and womb, and we will talk more. You are by yourself, yes?"

"Jonathan and Grace are at *our* table," came that nasally voice slicing through everything now, and Gracie almost choked as she gritted her teeth and forced herself to turn away from this man and look over into the gray eyes of Jean Baylor, who was standing like a silver spear of obstruction, hands on her slim hips, innocent look that was so fake Gracie wanted to applaud. "Shall we, Grace? We have *so* much to talk about!"

"Um, sure," she said, blinking hard as she felt that spell break as the man shifted on his feet and took a step back. He touched his chin for a moment, an almost puzzled expression on his handsome face as he glanced at her once more before looking over at Jean Baylor and smiling politely but not formally introducing himself.

"Jean Baylor Habib," said Jean to the man. She almost did a curtsey as she held her hand out like he was expected to kiss it. "I'm Abdul Mohammad Habib's first wife."

Surrogate for the Sheikh

Gracie almost doubled over as she choked back a sound that she wasn't sure would have been a snort or a howl. She caught the man hold back his own smile, and Gracie made sure not to make eye contact with him or she'd for sure burst into squeals, she thought.

"How many wives does Abdul Mohammad Habib have?" he asked with a seriousness that Gracie thought was admirably convincing. "Not eighteen, I hope? That is illegal even in the Islamic world."

"Oh, just me, of course," Jean said hurriedly, turning bright red as she touched her neck and then her hair. "I'm just so used to other Sheikh's wives introducing themselves as the first or second or junior or senior, that I just—"

"Ah, you are a Sheikh's American wife," the man said, touching his chin and frowning as he rubbed his stubble. "Sheikh Abdul Muhammad Habib? I apologize. I do not recognize the name. Of course, I am not so . . . as you say . . . plugged in as far as such matters go. I live on an island. Literally—we are an island in the Gulf of Oman!"

"Oh, no wonder I don't know you either," Jean said, deftly avoiding the question in a way that made Gracie want to just sit back and watch the performance. "You are . . ."

"I am . . ." he said, glancing slyly down at Gracie, raising one eyebrow in a way that made her want to giggle and wring her hands together like some of those ten-year-olds in her class. "I am going to kidnap your friend for the evening. Do not worry, I will return her by the end of the night. All of her. Red dress. Eggs. Womb. The entire ovulation ensemble of Ms. Grace Garner."

Now Gracie did in fact giggle and flutter her eyelids like she couldn't help it, allowing that tingling excitement to flow free as she realized they were . . . flirting!

"I hope you demand a king's ransom for my safe return," she said wryly, taking a step towards him, almost feeling a compulsion to take his arm and let him lead her away to his table, to his world, his island kingdom—which was almost certainly just beyond those heavy maroon curtains lining the side walls of the Grand Ballroom.

"A queen's ransom," he said. "Which is usually much higher than a king's ransom, because it is the lonely king himself who is paying to get his queen back."

Now he offered her his arm with a natural grace, like he was doing it without thinking. And she walked up to him, also without thinking, slipping her hand into the fold of his elbow, gasping under her breath when she felt the enormity of his bicep under that smooth black tuxedo.

"Careful," she whispered, glancing at Jean with wide eyes and then back up at this Arabian kidnapper in a tailored tuxedo that probably cost more than her car. "My friend's husband is the head of security in the land. A dangerous man. He might send his men after us."

Now the man frowned and half-turned towards Jean, his eyes narrowing for a fleeting moment, color rushing to his face along with a glimmer of recognition. Quickly he smiled and nodded. "Ah, now I recognize the name. Abdul Mohammad Habib. Mo Habib, yes? Head of Habib Security. I actually have an appointment with your husband later this week. My people do some business with him, though I have never met him. He does mention his wife to my people—in the most endearing terms, of course. Jean Habib. You have been teaching him English, I believe? Ah, my lady. I apologize for not recognizing the name earlier."

Jean blinked away what appeared to have started as a ferocious glare directed at Gracie, and she forced a smile and nodded graciously at the man. She didn't reply though, quickly looking back at Gracie, widening those gray eyes.

"So you and Jonathan *won't* be joining our table?" she asked sweetly, glancing once at the man and then back at Grace with the look of a college girl trying to stop a drunk friend from going home with the wrong guy—or with any guy. "We have two spots reserved for you, Gracie. We had to move things around a bit to get those passes and work out the seating, and if I had known—"

"I told you Jonathan wasn't coming," Gracie said as her jaw tightened. She remembered now that she had let Jean send her two passes anyway, and she felt a bit guilty when she realized that shit, it was pretty decent of Jean to reach out and invite her, and it was kinda lame of her to waltz off with some guy she didn't know instead of—

"Then I will join your table so those seats are not left empty," the man announced, now touching Gracie's hand and locking it tight against his arm as she stared up at him, incredulous at how forward this man was being, how openly he was . . . hitting on her! He looked down at her now, smile breaking wide, voice deep and commanding. "Come, Ms. Grace. It is not yet time for dinner. Let me show you the ice sculpture before it melts. Right now it is a swan, and in three hours it will look like a potato. Come. We must hurry!"

Now he *swept* her away in the ballroom, and Gracie tilted her head back and *laughed* as a breeze wove through her open hair, reminding her of that delicate whisper of his breath against her temple, perhaps inside her temple. Her feminine temple . . . hah!

God, this feels *so* good, she thought as she glanced up at the man, feeling a warmth and a chill, a tingle and a sizzle, her panties feeling tight even as her knees felt weak. So nice to be just straight-up *hit on* by a man who couldn't give a *damn* what the people around him thought! Not like how most guys were these days, almost apologetic even when they actually plucked up the courage to make an advance, like they were hoping the woman would relieve their anxiety and just take the lead in the courtship.

Not that Gracie had any problem with taking the lead in most areas of her life. Being a teacher was just a symptom of her need to be a director, a controller, someone who laid down the law and enforced it with a firm hand. So many parents these days practiced what seemed to be laissez faire parenting, Gracie thought, where they pretty much let the kids do what they wanted, rewarding them with praise and hugs, smiles and kisses. All that was good, and unconditional affection was important, but Gracie had always seen her role as being the authoritarian, and she liked to give the kids a sense of discipline, a sense that sometimes you just need to sit straight and do what the teacher says. No questions. No comments. I am in charge. I am the ruler.

And the kids loved it. They loved sometimes being able to not have to think for themselves and simply do what the teacher asked, trusting that she knew what was best for them in the classroom. Rules. Rules. Rules. Gracie the Ruler, they called her—which was an actual, real life thing now: wooden and thick, one of those old-style meter-rules which was about three feet long and had been nailed to the wall in her home-room as a parting gift from one of her classes.

They had painted the words "Gracie the Ruler" on the wooden rule, and Gracie had thought it was hilarious. Loving, witty, and hilarious.

But now Gracie the Ruler felt more like one of those kids lined up for a field trip as she held this man's arm and let him lead her through the maze of tables, the sea of heavily perfumed men and women wearing everything from Armani tuxedos to Arabian tunics, Middle-Eastern Sherwanis, and even an Indian saree or two. She glanced up at him once more as Jean Baylor faded into the background, and now it was just the two of them in an ocean of strangers, maroon velvet curtains lining the far walls of the hotel ballroom, chandeliers twinkling down at them as he swiftly led her across the carpet.

Grace could feel the hem of her red dress rise up as she was pulled along on his strong arm, the breeze generated by the two of them swirling its way up her skirts, kissing her bottom, teasing her tummy, tickling her tush.

"You are a teacher," he said as he pulled her off to the side of the ballroom, to a relatively uncrowded spot against those thick maroon curtains. They could see the ice sculpture in the distance. It was gigantic and gleaming, and it certainly wasn't going to melt anytime this century. "I am a teacher as well."

"Really?" she said, frowning up at him as she realized she was almost breathless from the excitement

Surrogate for the Sheikh

of being led through the crowd and tables like that, like she had just come off the dancefloor and was taking a breather before the next song began. "I wouldn't have pegged you for a teacher."

"Now *you* are being sexist," he said. "I am an excellent teacher, Ms. Grace."

"I didn't say that because you're a *man*," she said, swallowing as she tried to come up with a better way to say, "I said it because you look like a goddamn movie star, and I doubt any girl in your class is going to learn squat other than how to touch themselves. Perhaps touching themselves *while* they squat. Hah!"

"Then why did you say it, Ms. Grace?" he asked, turning to face her and stepping close.

Now she could smell him: a subtle cologne, his clean aroma mixing with the deep shades of fresh tobacco leaf, betelnut spice, red sage, the mix delightfully pungent, soaringly sexy, magnificently masculine. It made her reel for a moment, and she blinked as she wondered if she had eaten enough that day. Then she remembered that yeah, she had.

"Well..." she said, looking up at this exotic stranger whose name she couldn't remember and who suddenly seemed to be her date for the night. "I just..."

"You said it because you cannot imagine me as a teacher," he said, his voice low and steady, the vibration of the sound mixing with that manly musk in a way that made Gracie shiver as he stepped so close she could feel his heart, she thought. "Because as a girl you were never attracted to any of your teachers. Not like how you are attracted to me."

"Sorry, what?" she gasped, her brown eyes opening wide in panic before she narrowed her gaze and took a step back, not even sure where to begin. "*Excuse* me?"

"Do not panic," he said softly, now grazing his fingertips along the smooth white skin of her bare arms, his touch leaving a trail of goosepimples as he leaned close with those luscious lips of his. "I am attracted to you as well. There is no denying it. It is natural and beautiful. In the animal kingdom it is easy to see because the male and female go into heat only during certain times of the year. But in humans it is more subtle, and we have to trust our instincts to know when the timing is right."

Gracie frowned up at him in absolute *shock* as she felt the wetness ooze through her panties, the cooling flow giving rise to an internal heat that slithered up the back of her tingling thighs as she shifted on her feet again, spreading her legs ever so slightly.

Now from beneath her dress Gracie caught the slightest, most subtle scent of herself, her clean feminine smell, a scent that was pulling her arousal along with it, spiraling upwards through the ether like it was reaching out to him, to this man who was so close that perhaps he could pick up that secret scent . . .

And God, she saw his nostrils flare out, felt his

broad body tense up in a subtle way that she thought only she could see. Slowly he took a breath, filling his lungs as if he really *was* taking in her scent, and Gracie wasn't sure if she should faint or scream, step back or go closer.

What's happening, she wondered as she sensed movement at the front of the man's pants even though her gaze was locked onto his. It was like her senses were heightened to an impossible degree, like she could pick up every signal from his body, just like how she was certain he was picking up her warm scent from beneath the thin wet cloth of her black panties. Animals in heat? Timing and cycles? Eggs and wombs? Evolution and . . . ovulation?

Could it really be, she thought. I mean, I had my period ten days ago, so I'm probably right around that time when fertility is supposed to peak. And don't I teach my students about the mating cycles of animals, about how the female is more receptive at that time, how the male can sense when a female is peaking, how—

"Your friend was right," he whispered now, his voice low and hard, betraying a strain, like he was trying to control himself even as she sensed that movement in his pants again. "A woman is more likely to wear red when she is—"

And before he completed the sentence, and before Gracie could figure out what in God's holy name was happening, the man placed one hand firmly on the curve of her hips, grasped her wrist tight with his other hand, and in one swift move *whisked* her heavy body behind those thick maroon curtains.

Then he kissed her. Without asking, without explaining, without hesitating. He kissed her. He damned well kissed her.

3

"Are you insane?" she said as she broke from the kiss, pulling against his firm grip even as she felt his hardness pushing into her through his trousers.

"Yes," he said as he tightened his grip on her wrist, dug his fingers into the thick side of her bottom, and pushed her against the dark back wall as those heavy maroon curtains closed all the way around them. "I am insane that after I saw you from across the room, standing alone in that red dress, your curves calling to me in the most clear, undeniable way... yes, I am insane that I even waited this long to pull you into the shadows and take you, have you, fill you, claim you."

"Oh, my God, you really are insane," Grace said as she blinked and opened her eyes wide in the red-tinged darkness of the secret space behind the curtains. She tried to gather herself as the shock made her body feel weak and shaky, and she did her best to will herself back to that mental place where she could figure out the next logical step.

But there was no denying what her body was feeling, what her body was saying, what her body wanted, and the best she could manage was to just keep talking, to say whatever came into her head. "Insane. Mad. Completely off the rails," she said quickly. "But maybe it's a cultural thing and so I'm going to give you a chance to get out of this without causing a huge scene and getting the police involved. I'm going to count to three . . ." she said as she looked up at him, at that strong jawline that made him seem so self-assured it was lulling her into thinking that this was a perfectly sensible position to be in, that this man was in control and he knew what was best for everyone, what was best for her, Gracie Garner, mid-thirties and single, all alone in the grand ballroom, ovulating in her red dress.

"I'm going to count to three . . ." she whispered weakly as he leaned in and blew against her soft brown curls, his dark stubble grazing her smooth white cheek, his grip still tight on her wrist, other hand on her wide hips, his hardness undeniable

Surrogate for the Sheikh

against her thigh. "I'm going to count . . ." she muttered again, her voice trembling as the arousal snuck up along the curves of her bottoms, circled around the small of her back, slipped up through her bra, now teasing her nipples to silent stiffness, tingling its way up her neck, seizing control of her vocal cords and making them useless. Her mouth was hanging open now as she swallowed and swooned in his arms, those maroon curtains around them feeling like dark red clouds, like a cocoon, a place apart from the real world, the real world where Gracie Garner, schoolteacher and role model to little Oklahoma girls, would never even *think* about . . .

"I'm going to count to three," she managed to say one more time before all those thoughts got pulled down and smothered by her soaring arousal. "And then I'm going to let you kiss me again."

4

He kissed her again and she kissed him back, opening her mouth and sighing as she felt his warm, clean breath enter her even as his right hand moved around to her bottom and squeezed hard as he drove his tongue into her mouth. She could feel his arousal in the way he kissed her, the way he was growling against her ear as he firmly slid both hands under her dress from behind and grasped her bottom with such force she almost choked in shock.

Her eyes opened wide as she felt his fingers pull at the waistband of her panties now, pushing them down over her ass as he pinched and pulled at her naked buttcheeks, spreading them and squeezing as he kissed her neck with fury, all the while grinding his cock against her mound through his trousers.

"How rude of me," he muttered as he kissed her neck, now her cleavage, his tongue teasing its way along her creamy white skin, licking at the edges of her black bra even as he pulled her panties down past the heavy globes of her ass until they were stretched wide and rolled thin just above her knees. "To not formally introduce myself."

Gracie giggled and gasped at the same time as she felt his hands slide all the way up her dress from behind, pulling her asscheeks apart and running his fingers along the crack, now moving up along the smooth curve of her naked back, fingers deftly undoing the bra-clasp, releasing her swollen breasts as she gasped.

Immediately he lifted her dress and started to suck her boobs, pushing her back against the walls as she groaned and pulled at his thick dark hair, trying to block out those thoughts of how mad this was, of how there was a stranger sucking her stiff nipples behind the curtains of the Grand Ballroom in a hotel in downtown Tulsa, that a man in a tailored tuxedo was unzipping his trousers with one hand, rubbing her pussy with the other, lips firmly puckered around her left breast, mouth sucking hard and moving to the other boob, back and forth between her tits now, licking and sucking as he rubbed her mound from below, his tongue swirling its way around her large red nipples that were drawn up into tight points like rocky peaks of a desert mountain range.

"Incredibly rude to not introduce yourself," she muttered as she felt him slide two fingers into her cunt, the entry releasing a fresh flow of her wetness that told her she wasn't stopping, she wasn't going to make him stop, that every girl needs a release sometime, that there's nothing wrong with a one-night stand, that no one can see you and even if they figure it out, no one in this room knows you. Jean doesn't live here anymore, and who gives a shit what she thinks anyway. She probably already thinks I'm a slut for flirting with him, so to hell with her. I'm a good person and a great teacher and if I *choose* to let a man kiss me and touch me, it doesn't mean I'm a bad role model. That *was* the point of the sexual revolution, wasn't it? That a woman chooses when to have sex, with whom to have sex, and whether or not she wants to get . . . pregnant.

And now something the man had said when he first kissed her came back to her: "I will fill you . . ." Was his English not so good? Did he not know what that meant? Was he just saying stuff? Dirty talk? Did he just mean fill her with his cock? Or did he mean fill her with his . . .

And just as those thoughts all came rushing back,

thoughts of red dresses and ovulating women, eighteen children and surrogacy, renting out wombs and this man saying he wanted to "fill" her, she felt his naked cock spring out from his trousers and push against her thigh, and it felt so goddamn warm, so incredibly hard, and she swooned and swallowed when she looked down saw his tailored pants down by his ankles, crisp white shirttails hanging open, his cock *monstrously* erect, standing long and straight, hard and shiny in the smoky red light, thick like a post, heavy like a pipe, its gigantic head feeling hot and sticky as it teased the smooth white skin of her thigh, coating her goosepimples with the fresh ooze from its swollen, ready tip.

"Oh, *God!*" she gasped as she suddenly felt him grab the waistband of her panties with both hands and *rip* her underwear apart down the seams, now *slamming* her against the back wall and pushing her thighs apart, rubbing her wet slit one more time and then just straight-up *entering* her with his cock, pushing *hard*, pushing *deep*, driving *all* the goddamn way, thick and heavy, that swollen beast of a cock sliding up into her so quick it took her *completely* by surprise, forcing her mouth open wide like her pussy had just been stretched wide, her lips forming a silent scream of sheer *bewilderment* as she felt him *drive* the last inch of that cock into her as he grunted against her neck like a beast in heat.

"Ya Allah," he muttered as he grasped the meat of her thighs from behind and raised her left leg as his heavy, muscular body flexed full and held her in place against the wall. "You have made me insane, driven me bloody mad, turned me into an animal intoxicated by your feminine scent."

"Oh, God," she muttered as she closed her eyes and felt him drive up again, his cock somehow growing inside her with each thrust, his girth spreading her lips so wide it hurt in that most wonderful way, his length pushing into the deepest reaches of her cunt, the heavy head of his cock dragging against the front wall of her vagina with every pump, every pull, every thrust. "Oh, *God*, what's happening."

"*Ana sawf mmil' lakum,*" he muttered as he rammed his way into her, making her body shiver against the wall. "*Ana sawf mmil' lakum.*"

Grace could feel her arousal swirl its way upwards in a slow but determined spiral, the shock of what was happening adding to her heat, the madness giving it wings. Slowly she felt her body settle into his steady, powerful rhythm, and she let out a small gasp as she felt a quivering smile break on her round face. Oh, God, this feels so damned good, she allowed herself to admit as she focused on the incredible way he was filling her, the smooth power of how he was thrusting, his muscular haunches allowing him to withdraw almost all the way before pushing back in with a controlled power that felt forcefully lazy, seductively steady, pulling her body into his rhythm as she let out little feminine grunts each time he rammed his way back in, her pussy opening and clenching in synchronicity with his re-entry, squeezing tight each time he pushed back in, like her cunt was milking his cock in a way that made Gracie breathless with ecstasy.

Oh, God, my body feels so amazing right now, she thought as she became aware of electricity running through every fiber in her body, tingles crawling across every expanse of smooth creamy skin, heat soaring in every inch of her secret inner space that was being opened up and claimed by his cock, taken by his force, filled by his girth, explored by his length.

He thrust hard once more and then suddenly pulled out, turning her body and grabbing her wrists, slapping her palms flat against the wall as she yelped in shock. But Gracie let him guide her, and she kept her eyes firmly closed, smiling as she felt her pussy clench as it yearned to be filled again, like it knew that something was incomplete, that its job wasn't done, like there was still a hard cock to be milked to completion, coaxed to climax.

"Dhomaar," he whispered as he stepped back away from her and pulled that red dress off over her head, yanking that opened-up bra off as well until she stood there naked and spread, behind the curtains, palms flat against the wall, eyes still firmly closed. "Sheikh Dhomaar is my name."

"Pleased to meet you," Gracie muttered through her

stupor, feeling a smile break as she licked her lips and then gasped as she felt his hands slide down over her buttocks, letting her know the Sheikh had just bent down behind her upturned ass.

"Ah, my American schoolteacher," he whispered against her rear crack as he parted her buttcheeks and kissed her just beneath the bottom of her globes. "The pleasure thus far has been all mine, I fear But that is to change right now, I assure you. Now spread those magnificent American thighs wide for me. Spread for Sheikh Dhomaar, who is on his knees behind you. Spread for me, and I will make you come for me."

And as he said it he pulled her asscheeks wide, grabbing her globes firm and making her arch her back down to give him access to her slit from behind. Then with those buttocks spread wide, the Sheikh pushed his face between her thighs from behind and licked her along the underside of her wet slit, his tongue reaching all the way up to the front of her mound as she groaned and pushed into his face, moaning as she felt him ravage her pubic curls.

"Say my name," he growled as he licked her ferociously from beneath, kissing her buttocks, her inner thighs, his long tongue somehow reaching her clit as she arched down and spread so goddamn wide she could feel the air swirl like a cooling mist against her warm slit. "Dhomaar. Sheikh Dhomaar."

"Dhomaar," she gurgled as she looked down between her hanging breasts, gasping as she saw him squatting between her spread-out legs, his cock looking massive as it bounced gently as he leaned in and licked her again and again, his tongue sliding along her slit in the most erotic way as her pussy clenched and released like it had a mind of its own, needs of its own, instinct of its own.

"Dhomaar," she said again, and then she said it once more, and finally she could not speak through those trembling lips because he suddenly licked her one last time and then slid his stiff tongue deep into her cunt from behind and curled upwards with such unexpected force that she almost choked as her orgasm came smashing in like a hurricane in the night.

"That is only the beginning," the Sheikh muttered as he reached around and massaged her clit, pushing his tongue back in as he pulled her left buttcheek to the side, now smacking her bottom as her climax shuddered through her naked body. "I have waited six months for this, and you are going to be the focus of all that pent-up desire, all my stifled passion, all of me. All of Sheikh Dhomaar."

"What?" she muttered as she turned her head halfway and tried to focus. Tears from the strain of her climax were beading around the corners of her eyes, and through the watery haze she saw those heavy curtains billowing around her, the dark red making her feel like she was inside a womb in the clouds.

"*Ana sawf mmil' lakum,*" he growled against her naked back as he rose to his feet behind her, his hard cock brushing against her ass as he reached around and grabbed her breasts, pinching hard, plucking her nipples until they stiffened again to primal hardness. She felt the Sheikh guide his cock back to the entry of her slit, and as she swallowed and shuddered from the lingering ecstasy of that sudden orgasm, the Sheikh *pushed* back in and started to thrust *furiously*, pump *hard*, ram *deep*, so bloody deep, deep and hard, thrusting and grunting, again and again until he was straight-up *fucking* her, pumping her like a goddamn madman, a beast in heat.

"*Ana sawf mmil' lakum,*" he said again, and she felt his balls slap against her from behind as he went up on his toes each time he rammed back into her. Her arms were aching from pressing so hard against the wall, but she had to hold on or else his forceful thrusts would smash her face into the plaster, she feared!

"Oh, God," she gurgled, her voice wavering, the pitch rising and falling because of how hard he was taking her, how deep he was driving into her. She could feel his heavy balls slap against her again, again and again, in rhythm and time, like heavy clubs knocking on her secret doors as her pussy clenched in surreal delight, milking his cock in erotic glee, like her cunt was drawing his semen towards it, pulling his seed up along his throbbing shaft. She could feel it, see it, taste it, smell it, and every sense in her was alive as she felt the Sheikh pump and groan, thrust and moan, pulling her large nipples out into stretched points as she whimpered in pain and pleasure, now gurgled and groaned as he rubbed her throat from behind.

Now he reached down the front of her mound and started tapping her clit now, summoning her arousal as that sensitive nub stiffened and smiled from beneath its dark, swollen hood. "*Ana sawf mmil' lakum,*" he growled as he withdrew halfway, holding back now, flicking and tapping her clit as her whimpers spiraled upwards into a steady, droning wail. Slowly he pushed his heavy cock back into Gracie, flexing it in a way that pushed against the front wall of her vagina as she felt another orgasm start to build in the distance.

"Oh, shit, I'm going to come again," she gasped as her eyes flicked wide open even as the Sheikh's thick fingers rubbed her clit furiously while he pushed his cock deep into her with a slowness that made her pussy seize up like it was trying to hold him in there. "Oh, God, what are you doing to me? How can I be—"

"You are in heat just like I am," he muttered against her neck as he gently bit her earlobe, pushing that cock of his so deep she could feel it against the farthest wall of her cunt. "You are in season just like I am. Your body is yearning to receive just like my body is aching to deliver."

"What?" she whimpered, feeling a deep shudder go through her as he slowly sped up his thrusts while simultaneously slowing down the way he was flicking her clit, the reversal taking her so close, so close that she couldn't understand what he was saying, could barely understand anything except the fact that she was about to have another backbreaking orgasm, pressed up here against the wall, behind the red curtains of a hotel ballroom, naked and wet with a man she had just met. "Deliver . . . season . . . what?"

"Six months I have waited," he growled as he grabbed her by the sides of her wide hips and began to pump at full force, each thrust making those balls slap against her, knocking on her secret doorways, the entry to her womanhood, the anteroom to her womb. "Six months I have not orgasmed. Six months I have stayed hungry. My balls are heavy with my seed, full with the best of me, the best of my line, the best of Sheikh Dhomaar. And you will carry it. You will carry my seed. Grace Garner, schoolteacher at Wilson Park Middle School. Tulsa, Oklahoma. Grace Penelope Garner. All for you."

"Did I tell you my middle name?" she groaned through gritted teeth even though she couldn't understand why the thought had occurred to her through the madness of her arousal. But the words just swirled around her and disappeared, the ecstasy rocking her body and adding to the confusion even

Surrogate for the Sheikh

as the confusion itself raised her heat to the point of delirium, panic even, a hysterical feeling that the world was exploding into chaos, like the only release would be that climax, the only deliverance her orgasm, the only thing that would make sense would be her pussy getting filled with his load, that this Sheikh would fill her with his seed like how he was filling her with his madness, a madness that had her here, up against the wall, thighs spread wide, back arched down, heavy balls slapping against her, hard cock pumping into her.

And then suddenly *all* those words registered, *all* of it at once, and as the shock awoke her that orgasm *roared* its way in, *smashed* its way in, and she *thrashed* against him as those red curtains billowed with laughter, and she *flailed* in erotic agony as she came, and Grace *swore* she saw the face of the goddess riding the wave of her orgasm, felt the tongue of the goddess guiding the tip of his cock, heard the cackling laughter of the goddess in her own chokes and gurgles, whimpers and groans, sputters and moans.

And then she felt him come, by *God* she felt him come, those balls slapping one last time against her glistening underside and then *seizing* up, his thick fingers *clamping* down on her red nipples that were raw and aching, his cock *ramming* its way up into her one last time as he *blasted* his load into her depths, flooded her valleys with his milk, filled her wells with his waters, his thick semen flowing hot and heavy through the canals of her cunt as he groaned and grunted against her neck, muttering in Arabic, whispering her name in tongues.

He pumped her pussy and pinched her boobs as he continued to come, pouring more into her, and she could feel his semen pour into her, and she smiled as she took it, took it even as it took her, her own climax staying with their heaving bodies, her own orgasm stayed abreast with his, like two horses racing through the night, neck and neck, through the forests and into the sea, seahorses now, riding the waves of ecstasy, her orgasm now soaring to a crescendo and then shattering into a million secondary climaxes as she thrashed under his weight, shuddered beneath his strength, heaved with his heat, swooned from the sensation of his . . . his seed.

"*Ana sawf mmil' lakum*," he groaned as he finally thrust one last time and seized up, pushing the last of his semen into her as Grace felt her pussy clench up again to milk out that final load. "Six months for this. Ya Allah, it is done. It is done."

5
SIX MONTHS EARLIER
THE ISLAND KINGDOM OF MIZRA

"In six months it will be done."

Sheikh Dhomaar glanced up from where he stood looking down at the sandy waters that lapped at his feet. The salt water was not good for the leather shoes he wore, and they would need to be tossed away. Salt water was not good for anything that did not live in the sea, in fact, and these dead plants that surrounded what had once been a thriving oasis on the desert island of Mizra were now a testament to the cold ruthlessness of nature. This was the third oasis on the sprawling kingdom of Mizra that had been claimed by the ocean waters that also flowed beneath the island through a series of caverns and tunnels. That was the very reason the island was a desert: No fresh ground water to give life to the earth. But now even the scattered oases that had been enough to give Dhomaar's ancestors reason to take the island as their own were turning brackish as sea-levels rose around the world—or at least they appeared to be rising in the Gulf of Oman, whose salty waters were flooding underground caverns that had once lain empty.

"Six months, Dhomaar. And then you can go back to your whores and your harems, your sex vacations to Eastern Europe and South America. Do not act like it is the end of the world. It is actually the reverse, in a way. It is the beginning of a world."

Dhomaar turned from the dying oasis and looked over at his wife, the tall and thin Queen Zareena, her dark hair cut short to where she looked boyish in her long black robes, the traditional black hijab she always wore even though it was not required of the Mizrahi women.

"It is the end of my world," he growled as he strode past her and reached for a tall glass of fresh lemon juice that an attendant held out on a silver tray. He drank deep and slammed the thick-bottomed glass down on the hood of the silver Range Rover that served as the royal chariot when Dhomaar and Zareena ventured out of Mizra's capital city.

"Look around you, my Sheikh," Zareena said with a snort. "Your world is already ending. This oasis is dead, and that brings it to three oases that have turned to salt in the past two years."

"This oasis is small and remote," Dhom said. "We would never have needed its water anyway."

"It is a symptom of the disease that plagues our island," said Zareena. "A sign of what is to come. An omen of what lies ahead."

"You and your omens," Dhom muttered. "Why do you not use your magical powers to cast a spell and make the salt water turn sweet once more?"

"I do not believe in magic and you know that, Dhom," said Zareena, walking towards the massive silver car as an attendant hurriedly pulled the back door open for her. "And if I have any special power, it is to sense the patterns of the universe, the rhythm of the force that underlies all life, the signals destiny tosses in our way to remind us that there is so much we do not understand about space and time, so much we do not understand about ourselves, our bodies, the eternal spirit that lives in each of us."

"Ya Allah, your eternal spirit is hurting my head with this talk," Dhom grunted as he squinted towards the horizon, putting on his sunglasses and surveying the rolling dunes, the undulating curves of deep yellows mixing with smooth shades of orange, brown, and gold. The beauty of the desert was undeniable, he thought. But it was a harsh mistress, this land. It could not be broken, even though his ancestors had tamed it over the centuries, building a capital city around the grand oasis of Mizra, smaller towns and settlements coming up over the years, each of them located within a few kilometers of one of the smaller oases. Oases that would be useless in another decade or two, if the salting of the groundwater continued.

Zareena smiled as Dhom turned to her and began to slowly walk to the car. She waited until he got to the other side of the silver Range Rover, and then she winked at him. "If your head is cloudy from my words, then six months without sex, without orgasm, without release . . . it will bring back your clarity, my Sheikh. Semen retention is something all the great sages and mystics practiced as they walked the lonely path to enlightenment, sought their own version of nirvana."

Dhom finally grinned, thinking for a moment that yes, he did love this woman, though not in quite the way a man might love his wife. It was not a wholly sisterly love either, though the two of them had always been close, growing up as second cousins, raised within the marble and sandstone walls of the Royal Palace of Mizra. Their marriage had been arranged when he was thirteen and she only eleven, though the actual ceremony did not take place until Zareena turned eighteen.

Dhom smiled at his wife as he took his place beside her in the lavishly outfitted Range Rover, shaking his head at the way her strong jaw was set tight in her slim face. She was all business these days, though she had been blessed with a wicked sense of humor to go with that dreamy, mystical tendency that she seemed to be taking more and more seriously as she got older. Dhom had never understood that side of her, and indeed, he wondered at some of the decisions (decisions that defied logic but always worked out right . . .) she made as Sheikha of the land, a co-ruler to the king—just as the old laws had wanted.

Indeed, it was the old laws that had dictated their betrothal, Dhom reminded himself as he turned to the tinted window and gazed out at the barren landscape whipping by as the heavy car glided smoothly through the rough desert roads. Two tribes had formed an alliance to capture this island in the Gulf of Oman over a hundred years ago, and when the first laws of the Sovereign Islamic Kingdom of Mizra had been written, it was stipulated that the tribes would maintain equal power through the ages, through the generations. The end result of that principle had been the successive arranged marriages between the eldest son of one tribe and the eldest daughter of the other tribe. Both would be royalty, and they would rise to be supreme leaders and rule as Sheikh and Sheikha, king and queen, equal in every way. They would have children, of course. But the new Sheikhoods would not automatically pass to their children—instead the new Sheikh and Sheikha would be chosen carefully from amongst *all* the royal children of that generation, making sure to manage the complications of mixing the bloodlines too much.

It had been a departure from the traditional Islamic scriptures, and the Mizrahi law had brought with it other stipulations that banned the Islamic practice of a Sheikh taking more than one wife. It also prohibited the Sheikh and Sheikha from availing of the ancient Islamic provision of *talaaq*, a religious divorce. The ancestors were prescient enough to see that perhaps a time would come when a man and a woman united as teenagers did not want to be married anymore, and though that was acceptable for a commoner, such mercies were not to be afforded to those who bore the burden of supreme power. With status came the status quo.

And so it was that in the island kingdom of Mizra the Sheikh and Sheikha were bound for life, their duties to land and people superseding their private needs, their individual urges. But those urges were there, and those needs remained. Arbiters of Allah's will notwithstanding, the Sheikh and Sheikha were still of the flesh, and for this generation of Mizra's rulers, the needs of the flesh were too far apart for any hope of common ground.

Dhom had indulged those needs with reasonable discretion, preferring to pay handsomely for sex and secrecy abroad, forsaking the temptation of the women of his own land and even mainland Arabia. But Zareena's private needs had stayed closer to home.

Dhom glanced over at his wife once again as he thought of the first time he had walked in on Zareena with a girl. Dhom had just returned to Mizra after his first year at Eton College in England, and he had walked to the princess's private chambers unannounced, excited to greet his future wife, who was still just sixteen.

Sixteen but clearly quite grown up, Dhom had realized when he parted the lush purple curtains of her secluded evening-room and watched in shock, horror, and then amused wonder as his teenage cousin, his wife-to-be, the future queen of the land, gasped her way to a silent orgasm while grinding her crotch into the face of one of her young female attendants, the two girls naked and brown, glistening and beautiful in their forbidden embrace.

Dhom had kept her secret, even though by revealing it he could have saved himself from marrying a woman who would never want him sexually. It had not been an easy decision for a young, testosterone-filled man just entering his prime, the prince toweringly tall and strikingly handsome already, over six feet of heavy muscle by the time he graduated Eton, leaving in his wake a sea of European princesses screaming for one last taste of his Arabian manhood.

Yes, a hard decision, Dhom thought now as he watched Zareena take a phone call on her black headset, her sand-colored eyes narrowing as she barked at some poor minister in rapid-fire Arabic.

But of course he did not make the decision alone, he remembered as the domes and minarets of Mizra's Capital City came into view over the desert horizon, the gold dome of the Royal Palace gleaming in the afternoon sun, the tall white towers of the city looking hazy in the background, like it was all a mirage.

"Yes, it will be a mirage. Our marriage will be an illusion," that seventeen-year-old Zareena had said just two weeks before she turned eighteen, when she and the twenty-year-old Dhom were talking about what it would mean for them to go through with the wedding. "But all of life is a mirage, Dhomaar. We are all but wisps of smoke in the universe's candle-flame. We have a God-given duty to our land, to our ancestors, to our people. You and I both know that we are the only ones fit to lead Mizra into this new era, where our oil revenues will eventually weaken as the world moves to sustainable energy and our people face the strain of having to adapt to an economy that might actually require them to make some effort, some contribution. It will take decades of setting new policy, changing how we educate the children of Mizra, how we integrate our peculiar tribal Islamic culture with the global culture emerging out of humanity's shared values."

Dhom had rubbed his head at the time, still a bit shell-shocked at the reality of what he was about to do. But Zareena was right, and he knew it. With royalty came a burden, and there were truly no other princes or princesses that could take their places. If Dhom revealed Zareena's forbidden transgressions and refused the marriage, the succession would get complicated, since Zareena had no sisters and neither were there any other even remotely qualified female descendants of that second tribe in the current generation. Indeed, the family tree had dwindled over the years, and it was no longer a time when each generation saw thirty or forty royal cousins playing in the palace grounds. Dhom was the only real male choice, and Zareena was by far the most capable of the female royals.

So they had joined hands and taken the *nikaah* stage in the capital city of Mizra, the mirage of their wedding celebrated by the small island nation, their old parents beaming with pride as they watched their children take their rightful places.

For a decade Dhom and Zareena kept their secret,

avoiding the question of having their own children when their respective parents would inquire about the schedule for an heir—an heir that would, for the first time, be a *real* heir to the throne.

"The family tree has been shrinking over the generations," Dhom's mother would say during those discussions when both sets of parents would accost the young Sheikh and Sheikha after the morning meal, when the families would sit in the shaded gardens by the grand marble fountain.

"The bloodlines of the two tribes have been mixed and matched, diluted and distributed," Zareena's father would add. "We all carry blood from both tribes now. We are one people."

"And so we are getting to the point where it makes no sense to keep applying the old laws of ascendancy," Zareena's mother would say. Then, after some hesitation, she would add, "And as the number of children produced by each generation dwindles, we might soon be faced with the uncomfortable issue of . . . of . . . ya Allah, how to say it!"

"Inbreeding," Zareena would say matter-of-factly. "Eventually a child will be born with a beak and three tails."

"Perhaps scales and feathers," Dhom would add, raising an eyebrow and shrugging as the young Queen Zareena would stifle her laughter and nod very seriously.

Surrogate for the Sheikh

"We will need to put the children in cages instead of cribs," Zareena would sometimes say, and that would usually be the end of their elders' tolerance.

"You think this is a joke?!" Dhom's father would roar when it became obvious that Zareena and Dhom did seem to think it was a joke. "We are talking about the future of our nation, the future of our people, the survival of our unique variation of Islamic culture. And here the Sheikh and Sheikha of the land are making jokes about our line producing children with . . . *beaks!*"

Dhom would usually hold himself back from passing a last quip about his father's big nose which was very much like a beak. But he could not always resist the wisecrack, and those conversations often ended with both sets of parents losing their tempers and howling in Arabic as their twenty-something offspring left the room, passing each other secret looks of relief that they had avoided the topic for another few months.

But as the years rolled by and time had its way with all, Dhom and Zareena began to take those conversations a bit more seriously, and soon it was clear to them that their old parents were correct: Something had to change.

"It is time for Mizra to move to a more traditional system of ascendancy," Dhom's father had said in the later years, the man's voice weak with age, when it was clear the old generation were close to taking their places with the angels.

"Your brothers and sisters and cousins will not oppose it," Zareena's mother had said quietly.

"We have spoken with all the others of your generation who have children of royal blood," Dhom's mother had added with a smile that was part relief, part pride that perhaps her political skills were still sharp.

"None will oppose a change in the ascendancy laws," Zareena's father had said through his breathing tube as he coughed and sputtered. "Many have left the island and are settled in Europe or the Emirates, and they are happy with their status and their wealth."

"Ya Allah, it is almost sad," Dhom's father had growled. "Not even a whimper of protest. The oil money has truly made us all fat and lazy."

"But someday that oil money will be down to a trickle," Dhom's mother had said with a frown. "And the preparations for it must start now. Great changes will need to be made over the coming decades, and it is a blessing there will not be any disputes over the ascendancy to complicate things."

"So what are you saying?" Zareena had asked, her face twisting into a frown, those sand-colored eyes narrowing, her smooth brown face showing the fine lines of age even though she was just in her thirties.

"We are saying we have done the hard political work for you, my dears," her mother said, nodding

Surrogate for the Sheikh

at Dhom before turning back to Zareena and touching the queen's face tenderly. "Your first born child will be the undisputed supreme leader of Mizra, and from then on the line will stay fixed and clear. One heir. One line. It is done."

Dhom had frowned and swallowed hard the first time he heard the old ones say it. Zareena and he had discussed it before, but it was one thing to speculate and another to face the reality. The reality that they needed to have a child!

"The best of the two tribes is in each of you," Dhom's mother said, her old eyes tearing up. "After generations of intermixing, both of you carry the blood of our ancestors. And your offspring will consolidate that mix one last time."

"Or be born with three eyes and the beak of a toucan," Zareena had said to Dhom privately that night, when the reality of the matter had sunk in so deep that the joke brought a smile to neither's face. "That is a joke, but in a way it is not, yes? We still carry some of the same blood in us, Dhom. I know that cousins marry all over the world, and we are not even first cousins. But it does not feel right to me."

"To me neither, Zareena," Dhom had said. "But we have had our lineage tracked and analyzed by the finest geneticists. In scientific terms, we are about as related as two people meeting on Tinder in a medium-sized American town. The chances of some recessive trait emerging are next to zero. Ya Allah, look at our cousins and siblings. Look at us! All of us strong and healthy, smart and capable. Our parents are not fools, Zareena. Neither were our ancestors. All the marriages, all the mixing of the bloodlines, all the lineages have been meticulously tracked for the last hundred years. And since the 1960s our rulers have employed geneticists to analyze the records and advise us as the marriages were arranged. The science is there, clear as day."

"It is not all about science, Dhom," Zareena had said quietly, her eyes narrowing, jawline going tight as she met the Sheikh's gaze in the dark shadows of their private chambers, where they had slept on separate beds for the ten years of their unconsummated marriage.

"Ah, Zareena," Dhom had said, blinking and looking down for a moment before looking back into her eyes. "Zareena, there are other options. There is artificial insemination. It can be done privately, with—"

"It is not just that!" Zareena had snapped, her sudden flare-up surprising Dhom. But she had calmed herself down and smiled quickly, placing her thin brown hands in his meaty paws. She had felt like a baby sister to him in that moment, and a strange sickness had risen up in Dhom as she spoke. "It is not just that, Dhom. It is something deeper that tells me this is not right. I cannot explain it. It is just a feeling I do not yet understand well enough to put into words. Eventually that feeling will bubble up to where I can understand what the universe wants me to do. I know it. But right now it is just a feeling. A nagging sense that our coupling is not part of destiny's plan. That we are not destined to have a child. Some other solution will present itself. I am sure of it. We must wait, Dhom. We must wait and trust in the universe."

Dhom had nodded, relieved in a way. But as time had gone on, as parents had passed on, as both Dhom and Zareena progressed into their thirties, it became clear that duty and practicality would have to take precedence over hunches and feelings. And so after the last of their parents had been put to rest and grieved for, Dhom brought up the topic that could not be put off any longer.

"That feeling is still there, Dhom," Zareena had said. "But I am not so up in the clouds that I can ignore the practical matters. We need an heir. The country needs an heir. Time waits for no woman, and I do not have so many years left in which I can safely bear a child." She had sighed and looked down at her hands. "Perhaps I am wrong about that feeling I cannot express in words. Perhaps this *is* in fact the path the universe wants me to walk down." She had looked up and nodded, smiling gently at the tension that must have been obvious in Dhom's expression.

"Walk down with you, my cousin, my husband, my king, my fellow prisoner in this royal cage."

Dhom had smiled and hugged his cousin, touching her hair as he held back the annoying emotion that made his words catch in his throat. "I will arrange for the finest doctors to perform the IVF. It will be done in the comfort of—"

"No IVF," she had said, pulling back and shaking her head even as a chill rose in Dhom as he stared at his cousin, a woman who had never taken a man into her, never wanted a man in her. "If it is to happen, it must happen as nature intended. I am sorry if that is uncomfortable, Dhom." Then she had shrugged, that humor finding its way back into her eyes as she winked. "But trust me, it will be more uncomfortable for me. You can bring a woman in to get you ready, and then just before you—"

"Ya Allah, I get it, Zareena," Dhom had said, turning his face and placing a hand up between them as both of them broke into nervous laughter. "Of course it can be done, uncomfortable or not. But why put you through the unpleasantness? Millions of women have perfectly natural children through IVF, do they not? The science is—"

"Science! Ya Allah, Dhom! There are things about a woman's body that science is not prepared to even understand, let alone control. There are ways in which a woman's body opens up during sex, during climax, while being touched ... things that cannot be duplicated by the cold precision of a doctor in a white coat and latex gloves, using semen poured into a goddamn cup. I truly believe there are secret pathways, ancient instincts, deep wisdom of the female body that perhaps are not activated during a clinical conception, a fake fertilization. I know millions of women have given birth to wonderful children, *natural* children, through IVF. But I am of the old world. I must follow my spirit. No, Dhom. If we are to do this, then it must be done as Allah intended. I cannot argue about this any more."

Dhom had nodded in acceptance, steeling himself for crossing that line with a woman he had grown to love as a partner, for whom he had an affection not quite like that of a sibling but not like a lover's either. Still, Dhom knew himself well. There would not be any functional issues with getting the job done—no matter how many times he needed to do it.

Over the next six months they tried, the Sheikh and the Sheikha, with Zareena tracking her cycle, Dhom doing his duty. Zareena's private consort, her personal attendant who had committed to a life in the shadows of the Sheikha's bedroom, often held the Queen in a loving embrace as Dhom finished as quickly and carefully as possible, minimizing how much he touched his cousin, withdrawing and quietly leaving her chambers after delivering his load.

In a way this felt as clinical and cold as anything, Dhom had thought to himself. And sure enough, in the seventh month of it Zareena came to him one day with that look of resignation on her face.

"Bring the doctors," she had said finally. "Perhaps it is time for science after all."

The doctors came, and the doctors went. They drew healthy eggs from the queen. They collected royal seed from the king. But the fertilization failed three times over the course of a year, and that was enough for Zareena.

"No more," she had said defiantly when the trembling doctors assured her they had found the issue and *this* time it would work! "No more! I cannot ignore the signs. I will not ignore the omens. The universe has spoken, and I must listen to her silent whisper."

"What bloody signs? What goddamn omens?" Dhom had shouted when he learned that Zareena had sent the doctors packing, all of them laden with riches and the golden handcuffs of a non-disclosure agreement. "Ya Allah, Zareena. The hormone injections have driven you mad. You are imagining things that are not real. Oh, my Zareena, I cannot imagine the stress this must have placed on you. The strain on your body and your mind. The burden of—"

"It is our *duty* to handle stress and strain for the sake of our nation, Dhom. And you know that as well as anyone," she had snapped, folding her arms over her flat chest and rising up from the day-bed that faced the open verandah that looked east, towards the Great Oasis of Mizra. She walked past the Sheikh and onto the open balcony, placing her hands on the sandstone parapet and looking out at the date-palms that surrounded the waters of life. Now she turned, her eyes narrowed, jaw set. "But the signs are real, my Sheikh. Three months ago our surveyors reported that an oasis outside the city had turned brackish. They monitored the salt levels and found them rising over the next month. The oasis is now barren. This month another small oasis has suffered the same fate." She turned back and faced the sweeping vista of the Great Oasis that lay beyond the palace walls, its water still blue and fresh, clean and sweet. Then she whipped around, her eyes misty in the way Dhom had seen before and never quite understood, almost like she was in a trance, it seemed sometimes. "Our land is going barren," she said, touching her flat stomach and smiling wide, a strange glint in her eyes that made her seem mad for a moment. "How can there be a clearer sign that this is not the path of our destiny? That my feeling of something not right was indeed justified. That it is not in Allah's plan for us to have a child. For me to have a child."

Dhom had forced a smile and tossed his head back in a laugh that he knew sounded as fake as it was. "So what would you have us do? What is the succession plan for our kingdom when we are gone? Which of our wandering nieces or nephews does the universe want us to bring back home and saddle with the news that he or she will have to give up their life of luxury in the French Riviera and spend their days administering a boring island kingdom that no one has heard of?"

"Not so boring, and not so unheard of," Zareena had said sharply, that trancelike look quickly dissolving into the sharp focus that told Dhom she was back to being all business. "The Sheikh of Kalyan has heard of us."

"What?" he had asked, frowning and cocking his head to the side as he folded his thick arms over his heavy chest. "What does the blind old Sheikh of Kalyan have to do with us? Or anything, really." He snorted now. "He may be dead even as we speak! And besides, Kalyan is on its way to not even being a kingdom anymore, from what I hear. The Nawab of Kalyan is married to the sister of Sheikh Nasser, ruler of the great kingdom of Lihaal. And when the Nawab's father, the blind old Sheikh of Kalyan dies, Kalyan itself will eventually become a province of Lihaal. So what does Kalyan have to do with us?"

"That is *exactly* what it has to do with us," Zareena had snapped. "That blind old Sheikh is looking death in the eye, and in his twilight he sees visions of one last conquest. All day he mutters out loud in his chambers. He wanted his son the Nawab to engineer a takeover of Lihaal, as mad as that sounds now. It did not come to be, and now, his rationality blinded by the rage of humiliation, the old Sheikh is looking elsewhere in his madness. And we are on top of the list. I have it from a source in the Royal Palace of Kalyan. A man loyal to my consort here in Mizra tells her how the old Sheikh Kalyan speaks out loud to anyone who will hear!"

Dhom had laughed, and the laugh was real, booming, loud and resonant. He roared as he shook his large head, thick black hair billowing in the desert breeze as he put his arm around his queen and drew her close even as she pushed him away in annoyance.

"Spies in our neighbors' palaces? Rumors of an invasion? Our names on a blind old madman's hit list? Zareena, where is this coming from? What are you suggesting?! A mad Sheikh loading his war-camels onto barges and landing on the shores of Mizra under a full moon, taking the palace by storm, beheading the two of us and planting his wrinkled old buttocks on our throne? Ya Allah, my Sheikha! If you believe it, then you are as mad as you say he is! Your paranoia is truly rising to an admirable level. It must be a world record, in fact. The new world record in paranoia. There. Summon the Guinness Book!"

Zareena had laughed for a moment, but that sharpness never left her eyes—nor her voice. "No war-camels or beach-landings," she said with a quick smirk. "But the rest is possible."

The Sheikh had exhaled and rolled his eyes before

cocking his head as he focused on her. "What is possible? That the old man's arse is wrinkled like a prune? I concur, great queen."

Zareena scrunched up her nose and frowned away a smile. "Let me ask you this, Dhom. What would happen if the two of us were to drop dead right this moment." She whirled around on the open verandah, her flowing black hijab opening up and making her look like a dervish of Arabian myth. "Taken down by snipers from the far minarets."

The Sheikh squinted into the distance. "They would have to be very good shots. Military trained."

"It is a serious question, Dhom," Zareena said. "Plane crash. Heart attacks. Act of Allah's will. Let us say we are both dead tomorrow. What happens to our kingdom?"

Now Dhom had held her gaze, his green eyes widening before narrowing down to slits when he realized what she was saying. "Well," he began to say as his thoughts raced ahead, giving rise to a paranoia in him now. "Well, when our parents engineered those discussions with the rest of the royal family, they certainly mentioned that if the two of us were to pass without an heir, then indeed the burden would fall back to them. But our parents did not get so far as to specify *which* of the nieces or nephews would take over. They left it to the Royal Council to decide if the situation arose. After all, in thirty years who would know which niece or nephew would be most capable—and more importantly, most willing!" Now the truth of Zareena's point made his eyes go wide again. "Ya Allah, there is no clear line of succession! The laws have been changed to make it clear that our heir will be the undisputed Sheikh. But without an heir, there is no clarity. In fact there could be chaos! Especially if we are to die suddenly! The Royal Council would have to summon those scattered cousins and work through the mess of who will rise to the throne! We could put that in motion now as a failsafe, but the problem is . . ." He shook his head as he stared at Zareena, a strange fear rising in him.

"The problem is *none* of our cousins want the throne!" Zareena said, her jaw clenching into a grim smile as she tightened her arms over her chest. "Their wealth is secured, and they are all living their lives in adopted countries, pursuing their dreams or fantasies. Being summoned back would be a nightmare to most of them!"

Dhom had swallowed hard before stepping to the edge of the sandstone parapet, looking down over the fountains of the palace grounds, then towards the distant palms that marked the grand circle of the Great Oasis. "Ya Allah, Zareena. If we are to die tomorrow without an heir, Mizra would be a land without a leader. Of course, the Royal Council will administer the government as it does today. But a rule by committee would make the gears of government grind slow. The kingdom would lack the decisive power of a supreme leader."

"And it would also be destabilizing in a symbolic way that could add an air of uncertainty. In the old world such a situation would be ripe for an invasion," said Zareena, almost triumphant as her eyes shone like dark gold. She laughed now, shaking her head. "In fact that is the very history of Mizra, Dhom! The two tribes of our ancestors joined together to take advantage of *precisely* such a situation!"

Dhom took a breath and shook his head. "But that is the old world, Zareena. The world of today is too interconnected for an invasion to happen. Look at what happened when Iraq took Kuwait. That lasted a week, and Iraq is in shambles while Kuwait still thrives."

"This is *still* the old world," Zareena hissed back at him. "We are not on the map of the new world, and neither is the small kingdom of Kalyan. The West does not care because our oil reserves are just a drop in the bucket. We are not even a part of OPEC, by Allah. The world will barely notice if some island no one has heard of is invaded by some other inconsequential desert kingdom. You do remember that the one asset Kalyan has is a coastline. They have direct access to the Gulf of Oman, and you can laugh all you want about war-camels under a full moon, but Kalyan has always maintained a small but well-trained naval force."

Surrogate for the Sheikh

Dhom had taken a deep breath and rubbed his eyes. Zareena was getting to him, and for a moment he thought there might be something to her paranoia. Yes, the idea of an invasion in this day and age was ridiculous. But the blind old Sheikh of Kalyan was a ridiculous man! And Zareena was right: The United States and the West would not come charging in to save isolated little Mizra. The militaries of the West were already overcommitted, and small invasions were happening undisturbed and unnoticed every *month* in the shadows of Africa and the far reaches of the former Soviet Union.

"Remember, Dhom: Paranoia is the friend and ally of the great leader. All of this *can* happen. All of this perhaps *is* happening! So many coincidences, Dhom. Our inability to have a child. The warning from my consort's contact in Kalyan. And now our oases are turning to salt! *This* is how the universe speaks to us, Dhom! In coincidences and omens! Whether you think I am a madwoman or a witch, you know what must happen. We *must* have an heir in place soon. The symbolism is important. Even if the child is an infant when we die, he or she will be a stabilizing force because the Royal Council will be able to calmly administer the country until the child is of age. Just the symbolism of a royal heir could prevent this entire chain of events from ever happening!"

Dhom had rubbed his eyes and stretched his arms out wide, fists clenched tight as he looked up at the clear blue sky and then back at Zareena. "So you are saying what we already know, Zareena. We must have a child. So you must try the IVF again. Bring those quack doctors back or hire a new team. Whatever it takes. I will—"

But Zareena calmly shook her head, her eyes serene, her mind made up. "The blood of the two tribes runs in each of our veins. Either one of us carries the best of our ancestors, the blood of our forefathers and mothers. *You* will have the child, Dhom. That is what the universe is telling me. It is clear now. I am able to articulate that hunch now. Yes, *this* is what feels right to me. It must be *your* child, Dhom. You and a woman whom I believe destiny has already chosen and will be pulled into our sphere of experience as we proceed."

"A woman . . ." Dhom had said, frowning as he rubbed his stubble. "So . . . what . . . a surrogate?" He waited for Zareena to answer, but she stayed silent, eyes still serene, the focus still clear in them. He nodded and shrugged. "Yes. Of course. So we will find a surrogate. An Arab woman of noble blood."

Zareena snorted. "No Arab princess would agree to bear your child without becoming your wife, Dhom. And though I would agree to a divorce in a heartbeat if it secured the future of our nation, the laws bind us together until death."

Dhom had blinked as he looked at his co-ruler,

smiling and shaking his head before sighing. "You are right. A divorce would force us both off the throne. It would have the same effect as death."

"Correct," Zareena said excitedly, stepping forward as if the wheels were turning in her sharp mind. "And neither can you take a second wife. So that quite simply means we will never get an Arab princess to carry your child as a surrogate. Not a princess of any worth, anyway."

Dhom had frowned. "Any worth? What do you mean? What are you talking about, Zareena? What matter who the woman is? You doubt my masculine power? Ya Allah, my child will be strong and healthy, wise and powerful regardless of who the mother is! My seed is—"

"*Ayazisi*, Dhom. Yes, it is clear you are a bull, a stallion, an Arabian stud of the finest pedigree," Zareena said, shaking her head in mock exasperation as she stifled her laughter, tried to blink away that look of respect and admiration for Dhom as he stood before his kingdom and proclaimed his seed to be the best in history. "But it is not what I mean. I speak of the political aspect. The strategic aspect."

Dhom nodded and rubbed his chin as his sharp mind started to put the pieces into place even as he let Zareena speak.

"Yes, strategy and foresight. Because if my paranoid delusions do come to fruition and the two of us are killed while the child is still an infant, then . . ." Zareena began to say before trailing off for a moment.

"Then the child could be in danger. Having an heir would give stability to our government and people, but if we are targets, then certainly an infant would be an easier target." Dhom rubbed his dark stubble as his green eyes lit up with understanding. "So you are suggesting what? An alliance? The child also brings with it an alliance? An alliance between Mizra and the kingdom from which the surrogate hails?"

"A blood alliance," Zareena said quietly as the sun went behind a strangely isolated dark cloud. "If we are playing by the rules of the old world, then we must use the tactics of the old world, where children were important pieces of the puzzle. Alliances between nations forged by shared blood. By combining the bloodlines of two nations."

Dhom smiled and shook his head in marvel at the extent to which his wife had thought this through. But by God, it made sense! Certainly the chances of something as absurd as an invasion were low. But if it did happen, having a child with a woman from a powerful kingdom would by default make that kingdom an ally of Mizra. Old world indeed. By God, this woman was an able stateswoman!

"So we must choose a surrogate from a kingdom that would make a good ally in the case of any threat to our sovereignty," Dhom said, frowning as he blinked and narrowed his eyes. "What are you thinking? Certainly we can select a surrogate from any of the Arabian nations."

Zareena waved him quiet, a scornful look on her face, like she knew Dhom had already thought ahead and he just wanted her to say it. "That is pointless if she is not a princess. All the Arab nations of worth are Sheikhdoms, and unless the child is of royal blood, there will be no allegiance. No, we must look to a democratic nation, a nation that will go to war for even the lowliest of its people if it must!"

Dhom grinned now, one eyebrow raised as he looked at his cousin. "A democracy. The west? So we go to the top then? Is that what you are saying?"

Zareena smiled. "Yes, the greatest empire of today's world. The United States, Dhom. We must find an American surrogate. An American woman who will bear your child, carry our bloodline, secure our kingdom's future forever. That is where all of this is pointing, Dhom. Allah's guidance is strong and unwavering, and it has led us here. I believe *this* is why I was unable to bear your child. The universe twists and turns, but it always leads us to our destiny."

"An American surrogate," Dhom said, nodding his head. "Yes, OK. We can have our lawyers research a list of—"

Zareena almost spat on the clean sandstone floor of the open verandah. "*No!*" she shouted. "The future leader of our nation is *not* going to be born like that! The woman *cannot* know she is to be a surrogate. Not until she is pregnant."

Dhom almost doubled over as he snorted and stared at his cousin. "Are you mad, Zareena? What are you saying? I should . . . what . . . no . . . absolutely not. Think of what you are saying, Zareena! I should court some American woman, date her, tell her I love her, get her pregnant, perhaps even promise marriage so she carries the child to term and then, nine months later say sorry, you are just a vessel for my child? Then what? We write her a check and tell her to hand over the baby? Is that not the plot for the movie the Omen? Are we trying to seed the Antichrist or the future leader of our people?! By God, I have angered some women in the past, yes. But something like this could get me killed faster than a hundred archers on their war-camels! Enough, Zareena. Everything made sense until this. Absolutely not."

Zareena sighed and shook her head. "I am not suggesting months of courtship and romance, Dhom. That would be deception, and it would defeat the purpose. No, the conception must occur on the very first meeting."

"What? Hah!" Dhom had said, eyes wide in disbelief. "Sex on the first date?" He chuckled. "Though now perhaps we are entering the world of Sheikh Dhomaar!" he said, offering a wry smile at his joke.

Zareena smiled, her eyes narrowing mischievously

Surrogate for the Sheikh

as she looked at the Sheikh. "I am serious. The woman must be under no illusion that this is anything more than one night of passion with a mysterious, virile, exotic man. Yes, Dhom. You must seduce her on the first meeting. Take her that very night. Fill her with your divine seed, you Arabian stallion. Hah! You can handle that, can you not, my Mizrahi bull?"

Dhom had *roared* with laughter, stretching his arms out wide as he stood and faced his kingdom, beating his club-sized fists against his mammoth chest as Zareena laughed along with him, the two of them howling into the blue sky that was slowly fading as the day wore on.

They laughed it out, but then it was business again, and Dhom settled down and turned to his wife once more. "Even if I am to agree with this madness, to impregnate a woman on the first try is leaving a lot to chance, is it not? Yes, my power and virility flows strong like the rivers of Babylon, but I cannot deliver if a woman is not ready to receive. Pregnancy is about two people. So am I supposed to run around New York City having sex with countless women until one of them gets pregnant? What if they all get pregnant? What if none of them gets pregnant? It is not that the job wouldn't be pleasurable," he grunted, shrugging as Zareena rolled her eyes and made a face. "But so much unprotected sex with unknown women... it seems like we are asking for trouble."

Zareena shook her head quickly, her expression

signaling she had already thought this far—perhaps further even. "It will be one woman. She will not be unknown. And you will seduce her at precisely the right time."

Dhom laughed again. "Ay, you are mad, Zareena. So you are saying we will select some American woman? Have her followed? Track her cycle? Then send me in with my cannons blazing just when she is peaking? Is that not cold and calculating—perhaps even more so than just having our lawyers approach surrogates and come up with a list?"

Zareena shook her head. "You will do none of that. No selection. No stalking. No tracking. That will be my job. Your job is only to be prepared."

"Hah!" Dhom said. "I am always prepared, my little cousin. Why, just last month I had the Madam of my Las Vegas club throw up her arms in despair and say that her girls cannot take any more even though they want to! My queen, I am always prepared!"

"Not like this," Zareena said. "It will take all of your iron will, my Sheikh. All of it."

Dhom frowned as he watched Zareena's eyes twinkle with a strange look. Not quite satisfaction. Not exactly mischief. More like a challenge. A serious challenge.

"No," he muttered as he saw her thin red lips curl up at the corners. "Ya Allah, you cannot be serious."

"Six months," she said. "You will gather your strength for six months. No women. No sex. No orgasm. Not even by your own hand. You will even control your goddamn dreams."

"This is a joke," Dhom snorted. "What is the point? Maybe I hold off for a day or two before. But—"

"The point is by letting your energy build up, you will be peaking at the same time as the woman I choose," Zareena said. "The woman will be at peak fertility, and your need will be so raw and primal that neither of you will be able to stop yourselves. The ancient wisdom of the body will take over. The same instinct that leads the alpha beast of the jungle to walk a hundred miles to seek a female in heat. The seduction will be done by the signals your body sends out. The very scents emitting from the heat of her sex will ignite the deepest need of your sex. It will maximize the chance of pregnancy on the first try. It will virtually *assure* it." She had paused and taken a soft breath as that glazed look returned to her eyes. "Yes," she said. "This feels right to me. This feels like the way, the path, the road to our destinies. To your destiny. To our kingdom's destiny. And to the destiny of this American woman."

Dhom had taken a deep breath as he let all of it sink it. It had begun to make some sense in the strangest of ways, like he could feel a calmness in his body. It was as if Zareena was correct. This did feel strangely ... right! This did feel somehow preordained. Destiny? Or nonsense? Who knew?

"So you do not want me involved in the search for

this woman," he said finally, drawing another breath of the desert air that seemed to have a new ingredient in it. "You want my meeting with her to be truly spontaneous for both she and I. You want the attraction to be real. The passion to be genuine. The need to be raw and undeniable for both she and I."

"Yes," Zareena said quietly, her eyes softening for a moment as she squeezed his massive upper arm and touched his face affectionately. "And it will be real. I feel it. Whoever she is, she will be the real thing. For one night, at least."

Dhom grunted. "OK, Zareena. All right. Let us proceed. I will do my part for my nation, like I have always done." He looked down at her now, eyes narrowing as he smiled wryly. "But just out of curiosity—since it appears you have thought this through: How are you going to engineer this? You have spies in America now, just like in the bedroom of the blind Sheikh of Kalyan?"

Zareena laughed. "I do not have *spies* anywhere. The Kalyan connection is through my woman Alma." She laughed again before shaking her head and blinking. "As for the United States . . . well, I actually might have spies there, now that I think about it."

Dhom raised an eyebrow and leaned in, grinning as he rubbed his large hands together and waited. "Ya Allah, this is bloody exciting! Go on, dear queen! Tell me about your elaborate game of chess, where you control the board and all the pieces!"

Zareena shrugged, her jaw tight. "Sheikh Nasser's former Head of Security," she said softly. "He married an American woman and now runs a private security company in California. He is discreet and reliable. He has the resources, or can find them. I have already laid out my requirements, and he has already come up with a list of women who will be tracked over the next six months."

Dhom's eyes went wide as he stared at Zareena. But of course she had already gotten things in motion. Why should he be surprised? Combine paranoia with "signs from the universe" and perhaps a few hormone injections and there you have it! Ya, Allah, guide me through this mad but certainly intriguing journey!

"How did he come up with this list?" Dhom said after swallowing hard and deciding to keep the conversation on point.

Zareena stayed deadpan. "He logged into his wife's Facebook page. Pulled up all the women who met the criteria I gave him."

Dhom snorted, eyes going wider. "And those criteria are?"

"Between twenty-eight and forty-two. Unmarried. No other children. Not using birth control. No complicating medical history. Low-paying job and no family money. A psychological profile that would make it very unlikely that she would consider an abortion if things got complicated. And a selfless personality that would eventually choose the child's best interests over her own. Still, it could get complicated unless you follow my instructions to the letter. One night and one night only."

"Complicated?" Dhom said with another snort, folding his arms over his chest again. "Like how?"

"Never mind," she said quickly. "Just my paranoia, dear husband. Anyway, these women are being tracked already." She shrugged. "In three months we will have a picture of their cycles. In six months we will be able to know with virtual certainty when each woman is ovulating. By then some women will have been eliminated from the list. When we have narrowed it down to one woman, Habib will orchestrate an event at which both you and she will be in attendance." Zareena shrugged again. "And then nature will take its course, my raging bull. The rivers of Babylon can flow again!"

"Ya Allah," Dhom muttered, blinking through wide eyes as if he had been staring into the sun. "I feel like nothing more than a gigantic pair of balls in your game of human chess!"

Zareena laughed. "Trust me, great Sheikh. After six months of restraint, you will indeed *be* a walking pair of balls!"

And they both laughed again as the sun finally sank behind the sandstone skyline of Mizra, that gray cloud ambling by in the darkening sky as this king and queen made their plans. They hugged once, still laughing but both feeling something in the air, like their decision had indeed set a chain of events into motion, the destinies of many merging into a peacock swirl of color, space and time shrinking down to that cosmic eye within which the god and goddess dance their ritual dance, the prelude to the divine mating that creates from what it destroys.

"Who is this former employee of Nasser's who is married to an American?" the Sheikh asked as they finally strolled back into the palace to prepare to hold court before dining with the ministers.

"A big hulk of a man who does not speak much," Zareena said. "Abdul Mohammad Habib. He married an American schoolteacher—though she will know nothing of this plan."

"Schoolteacher?"

"Yes. Jean Baylor is her name."

6

Jean Baylor smiled tersely and touched the back of her neck as Gracie excused herself and slipped into her seat at the round table towards the far corner of the Grand Ballroom.

"Gracie, this is my husband," said Jean, holding that terse smile. "He's actually the one who asked if I had any old friends in Tulsa I wanted to invite to this exclusive gathering! May I present to you Abdul Mohammad Habib of Lihaal."

"Habib," said the gorilla-sized man with the thick beard and the impossibly dark sunglasses that made it seem like he was Stevie Wonder's evolutionary ancestor—or at least his style guru. "Just Habib."

"Pleased to meet you, Habib," Gracie said, smiling wide but staying seated as she noticed Jean eyeing her up and down. Gracie was sitting with her thighs held tight together, just minutes after emerging from behind that curtain with (or rather, without . . .) a torn-in-half pair of panties that Dhomaar had thankfully taken care of (which was only right, considering he was the reason they were now useless). Dhom had stayed behind the curtains so they'd walk out separately, and Gracie had shuffled over to Jean's table, her face as red as her dress, those thighs clamped together so the Sheikh's semen wouldn't run down her legs while she walked!

Oh, *God*, this is insane, she had thought as she imagined a million judgmental eyes on her. Ohgod, ohgod, *ohgod*!

"Um, Grace," Jean whispered now, those gray eyes of hers glancing at Gracie's cleavage so hard that Grace had to fight to not look down to check if her boobs were hanging out or if there were bite marks all over her smooth skin. "Yes, so it's fine to be casual with my husband, of course—but when I introduce you to the other guests who'll be joining us at the table, could you rise to greet them? Some of them might be royalty, and it's just—"

Habib grunted loudly and swiped at the air with his hairy paw. "There is no need. Very little royalty in room. Mostly American Arabs. And no royalty at table. Two of my employees only. Only royalty will be *your* guest, Ms. Garner—as my wife tell me! Hah! See, Jean? Because of your friend *we* are to spend the evening with royalty!"

His accent was hard to understand, and Gracie just nodded and smiled earnestly as she took a moment to process the words. She glanced at the empty chair next to her, doing a double-take when she saw a namecard with Jonathan's name printed on it. Shit, she thought. She wanted to grab the tag, but she decided not to do it with Jean's eyes on her. Already Jean could sense something was up. God, perhaps Jean could *smell* that something was up . . . up inside Gracie's—

Stop, she thought in a panic as she felt her pussy clench almost in reflex, the way it had been doing all through that *insane* session behind the dark red curtains. It was so strange how her body had reacted to him, so freaky how fast her arousal had soared, so weird how her cunt literally seemed to be operating independent of her brain, like her pussy was seriously trying to hold the man's semen inside its depths!

God, was she crazy?! It was bad enough to get so caught up in the moment that you let him come inside you, she told herself. And now look at you. You're sitting here holding your thighs together, clenching your pussy like some . . . some . . . oh, God, what *are* you now? A slut, or something worse? What if you get *pregnant*, Gracie?! From a *stranger*?! A *for-*

eign stranger whom you know *nothing* about?! And did he say he was a *Sheikh*?! So now she could be pregnant by a foreign, stranger Sheikh. OK. Move along. Nothing to see here. Oh, *God* how could this happen?!

Calm down, she told herself. Nobody gets pregnant the first time they have sex with someone, right? And she could always take the morning-after pill if she was still freaking out tomorrow.

Could she take that horrid pill, though? she wondered suddenly. *Would* she take that pill?

There was no denying that Gracie wanted a child. She knew she was destined to be a mother—perhaps several times over. Hell, that's why she had left Jonathan. She hadn't consciously analyzed the change of heart about Jonathan that happened so suddenly at the diner—even though it hadn't escaped her notice that it was strange how much her body seemed to be controlling her emotions. It was like the need to have a child was dictating the kind of men she was attracted to, and letting her walk away from the others without a second thought!

And *God*, it was attraction she felt for this new man, this beautiful hunk of a man, this Sheikh Dhomaar. Those broad shoulders. That towering height. The rock-hard bulk of his chest and arms. That strong, incredibly defined jawline. And those green eyes!

Is this a dream? Did that really happen? Is this man even real? Or was that red curtain a gateway to some alternate universe, where I just had sex with a god who wanted a taste of a human woman. The Greek gods used to do that, right? Same with the Indian gods and goddesses. Yeah. Sure. That's probably it, Gracie.

She glanced at that empty seat again as a curly-haired man and a wiry, dark-skinned woman walked over to the table, the woman looking at Grace like they knew each other. Or at least like she knew Grace.

"Hello! I'm Grace Garner," she said, relieved to be taken from her thoughts that were swirling round and round faster and faster, spinning her mind into a dizzying web of disbelief and distress, excitement and paranoia, guilt and . . . "Do I know you?" she said way too loudly as the wiry woman leaned over and shook Grace's hand, making hesitant eye contact, almost like she was embarrassed.

"They are my employees and they not know good English," Habib said gruffly, glaring up at the woman as she hurriedly nodded and sat down, pulling out her phone and staring at it. "And they are on the clock. No idle chit chat, yah?"

No idle chit-chat, Grace thought as she glanced at that empty seat next to her and wondered how the hell she was going to carry on a conversation with Sheikh Dhomaar while Jean stared her down. Hell, what would she say to this man even if Jean *weren't* here?! What do you say to a stranger whose semen is still inside you?! How's the steak? Pass the bread? Oh, my God. Ohmygod. Oh. My. *God*! I can't do this! Oh, God, Jean's going to see it the moment he shows up! It's going to be all over Facebook! My students are going to see! The principal is going to see! I'm going to be fired! Then I'll be broke! And pregnant! And . . . and . . . and . . . *stop*!

And Gracie the Ruler managed to control herself, and she forced a smile and began to engage in that idle chit-chat with Jean even as her mind stayed on the empty seat next to her.

The empty seat that stayed empty as the wine was served, that stayed empty as the salad and bread arrived, stayed empty as the main course landed, stayed empty through dessert and coffee. Empty . . .

Empty like that strange, sinking feeling in Gracie's stomach. Empty like her life inexplicably felt right now. Empty.

7

"This is *empty*!" roared the Sheikh, tossing the silver metal cup across the wide back seat of the stretch limo that was pulling away from the Rega Royal Hotel in downtown Tulsa. "I asked for a bloody cup of sweet tea! Am I not still Sheikh here?! I will have you bastards beheaded, your families executed, your remains fed to your camels. Then I will execute your camels and eat *them*! Ya Allah, I am going *mad*!"

"Good," said Zareena, calmly watching him from the safety of the far side of the limo. She was still in her black hijab, a sequined veil covering her nose and mouth, black eyeliner on. She had not entered the hotel, instead choosing to wait in the limousine

Surrogate for the Sheikh

in the private underground garage. "Your rage is the sign you were successful."

"No, Zareena," the Sheikh said through gritted teeth as he tried to control an energy that threatened to overwhelm him. "My rage is a sign that I am *angry*! Simple as that, you damn woman! Will you *stop* it with your goddamn signs and omens! Ya Allah, stop this car so I can *smash* something! And where is my goddamn *tea*!"

"There is a public park in one kilometer," Zareena said to the terrified driver, who seemed unsure whether or not to raise the bulletproof partition to protect himself from the Sheikh. She tapped her phone and nodded. "It will be open until midnight, and should be secluded enough. Stop there, and let our Sheikh smash something."

The driver almost swooned in relief as he nodded and sped up before slowing down and pulling over. The Sheikh did not wait for the bodyguard to open his door—he barely waited for the car to stop moving—and within moments he had burst out into the open, ripping off his thousand-dollar bow-tie and tossing it, undoing the top few buttons of his shirt as he ran along the dark grass like a madman, a crazed energy flowing through him, a manic force that made him want to *roar* to the heavens, *smash* his fists into those silent tree-trunks, *rip* those lamp-posts out of the ground and bend them around the goddamn world itself!

"What is happening to me?" he panted as he finally stopped running and turned around to see Zareena standing there in the moonlight, her black hijab shining silver in the half-moon, those sequins on her veil glimmering like stars from the light reflecting off a small duck-pond to their left. "Ya Allah, I feel calmer now after letting out some of this energy. But by God, Zareena!" He snorted with incredulous laughter as his green eyes went wide. "For a moment I thought perhaps I was turning into a werewolf, some kind of beast-like transformation."

Zareena calmly glanced at the moon. "If I remember those movies, you would need a full moon to turn, dear Sheikh. But not to fear. I would make the sacrifice of putting a silver bullet into the beast to save you from a life of torment. Especially now that you have passed your seed on."

Dhom grinned as he finally gathered himself and realized he was soaked in sweat, almost like a fever had broken. He felt alert and alive, powerful and manly. But there was something else he felt. A strange, gut-wrenching, *empty* feeling. Like something had been taken away from him. Like a part of him had been ripped away and left behind. A part of his body. A part of his very s—

"Passed my seed on," he repeated, exhaling hard as he took his jacket off and stood with his hands on his hips. "Ah, so this inexplicable burst of madness is just the end of a release that has been building up for six months. Yes, of course. It has been so long without a woman that I had forgotten how a woman can make a man feel like a goddamn *animal*! A *beast*! A bloody *king*!"

"I will take your word for it, Dhom," Zareena said with some amusement as she carefully removed her veil from one side, letting it hang down against her left breast. "Yes, I would expect that after six months of holding back, tonight's release has driven you a little mad—which is all right, of course. It is natural. You have seen how the male animal frolics like it is possessed by a demon after it has taken its mate. But it is not just that animal instinct. It is something else, something very human. It is fascinating to see, actually. Ya Allah, it is fascinating to see it at play, how it actually—"

"So now I am some animal to be observed for your fascination," Dhom said, grinning as he looked around at the grove of silent elms, the pond with its lily-pads and curious frogs, the hedgerows lining the paved paths, painted wooden benches symmetrically placed, all bearing silent witness. He held his arms out wide, flexing his muscles in a way that made him feel damn good—though that strange pit in his stomach still nagged at his peace in the most annoying manner. "So observe. Take notes. Ask questions."

Zareena smiled a little, her eyes narrowing as she took a step and then folded her arms across her chest. "OK, Dhom. Here is a question. Even though your body feels alive and strong, powerful and virile, do you feel something else?"

Dhom swallowed as that emptiness reared its head as if it had been called by name. "Something else like what?"

Zareena shrugged, blinking and looking down at the dark grass for a moment. When she looked up her eyes were slightly glazed over again, that trancelike look returning. "Like perhaps something is missing. A feeling of . . . of . . . yearning, perhaps. Yes?"

Dhom grunted and turned away as that feeling rose up like a specter from the shadows, its dark fingers wrapping themselves around him from the inside, squeezing at his core in a way that almost made him sick. His jaw went tight now, eyes narrowing, mind swirling like a roulette-wheel in spin, spinning images and emotions, fears and fantasies, visions and wisdom, spinning again, faster and faster until it abruptly stopped, drawing all those images and visions, emotions and energy down to a single point, a single image. Her.

Ya Allah, the Sheikh thought, slowly turning on his feet as he sensed that feeling inside him literally reach up and grasp at the mental image of this woman, Gracie Garner, this curvy American woman who had feel so *damned* good against his body, felt so *bloody* warm against his skin, felt so *goddamn* perfect around his cock!

He looked at Zareena now, his majestic face twisting into a frown that was part confusion and part realization—realization that Zareena was right. The feeling inside was indeed like . . . like *yearning*! But why? He barely knew this woman! He had slept with countless unknown women in the past, and surely this feeling would have emerged before, yes? But no. This was new. It surprised him. Shocked him. Damned well *terrified* him! What if it did not go away? How in Allah's name—

"It is the human need for pair-bonding," Zareena said now, her voice quiet and steady, betraying some tenderness but with an undercurrent of concern. "Many animals bond in pairs, but in humans it is heightened to a level that goes beyond the physical, that reaches to that place deep inside the human spirit, the seat of the soul, the source of the god and goddess that lives inside us. You have denied yourself that feeling your whole life, committed to our mirage of a union and keeping your private needs in the realm of the physical. But this one coupling with Grace Garner has awakened that feeling in you, Dhom. That desire to bond with one person, form that divine union with a woman. Indeed, I expected it, yes. But not to the extent that I am seeing in you. Ya Allah, it is beautiful to see, but also concerning. It must be killed before it sinks us all."

Dhom swallowed as he felt his stomach go tight, the

muscles in his torso flexing like thick cords of steel. "Pair bonding," he said slowly, rubbing the stubble on his chin. "So this feeling will go away?"

Zareena nodded quickly, blinking as she broke eye contact. "Of course," she said. "But it is best you go away as well."

Dhom frowned. "Back to Mizra already? I thought the plan was to remain in the United States for a few weeks while Habib's people keep track of . . ." He swallowed hard as her name caught in his throat like she actually meant something. "Keep track of the woman," he finally said, steeling himself as he realized that by God, perhaps he *did* need to go away and clear his head. Because if he didn't, if he stayed here in Tulsa, just a limo-ride from her, then . . . then it would be *damned* hard to not take that car-ride. Damned hard to not take *her*! Again and again!

Ya Allah, I want her again, he thought. His cock moved in his pants now as he felt a spark of energy, that emptiness momentarily transforming to elation, like a part of him was saying, "Yes, yes, *yes*! We *must* go to her again! We *must* have her again! She is *ours*, Dhom! She is *yours*, Dhom! Take her again! Take her now. Bloody hell, take her forever!"

"You will not need to see her again, I believe," said Zareena slowly, studying his expression with those sharp eyes of hers. She tilted her head slowly now, looking past Dhom and towards the dark blue night sky. " And so I do not think you need to be here. Something tells me you have done what you needed to do. I believe the power of your reaction is a sign she will conceive from tonight's coupling. I think that is why you have reacted so strongly to being separated from this woman. A man feels a need to protect the woman who is carrying his child, just like the woman feels a need to remain with that man. It is done. Ya Allah, it is done, and you must separate from her. So go, Dhom. Go and clear your head. Clear your body. It is done, and now I will handle it. I will stay in Tulsa and coordinate with Habib's people. They will watch her and keep me abreast."

Dhom nodded silently as he clenched his fists and looked towards the dark street on the fringes of the park. He nodded again as he began to walk back to the limousine, his mind slowly coming under his control even though his body still held on to that sickening feeling, the sense of yearning that he hoped would go away soon. This had always been the plan, he knew. One night. One try. One time. Make it count, Sheikh. There would be no further contact between the Sheikh and Grace. As far as Grace was concerned, it would be a one-night stand that resulted in a pregnancy. A spontaneous sexcapade. A frivolous fling. An exciting episode with a mysterious stranger. She would perhaps be a little hurt, but certainly in today's America it was not a shocking thing to have a one-night stand, yes? She could not have expected anything more given how things played out, yes? Just one night of anonymous passion! These days so many women actively sought such encounters!

Not this woman, though, the Sheikh knew. Of course, he did not know anything about her other than her name and the fact that she was a schoolteacher. Zareena had wanted their meeting to be genuine, spontaneous, unrehearsed as far as possible. And by Allah, it had worked, had it not? It did not feel like meeting Gracie was part of some devious scheme to hijack her womb! It felt like . . . like . . . by God, it felt like some *other* kind of plan! God's plan? Destiny? Signs from the universe? Was he going mad and starting to believe Zareena's nonsense about angels and cupids, dancing fairies and giggling gnomes, all of them playing a hand in our lives at the behest of the gods and goddesses, the puppet-masters playing their games? Ya Allah, madness indeed!

Was it though, the Sheikh thought as he stood by the limo and watched Zareena calmly step to her side of the car and give him a strangely knowing look before getting in. Yes, was it all madness? Or was there something to all this stuff Zareena believed in. That even though they were planning and scheming, there was also the plan of the universe at play. All of her "this feels right" and "this feels off" and so on and so forth? Does she not simply mean to say "this feels in line with God's plan" or "this seems to be where the universe is leading us?" And is that not the same sense I am getting as I feel this strange yearning for this woman?

Now something occurred to the Sheikh as he got into the car, and he frowned and then suddenly flicked his eyes wide open as he glanced over at the Sheikha.

"Zareena," he said softly, doing his best to keep his voice steady even though that crazed energy was beginning to surge again.

"Yes, Dhom?" she said, that look still in her eye.

"It just occurred to me that you never actually showed me a photograph of this woman before sending me into that ballroom. You gave me her name, yes. But that is all. You did not give me any way to actually find her in a crowded room," he said, his voice wavering as he tried to stay calm and not panic as if the world suddenly did not make any sense to him. "She was by no means the only pretty American woman in the room. Perhaps she was not even the prettiest one! But I noticed her immediately. I went to her without thought. Why did you not think to show me a picture beforehand, Zareena?"

"An animal does not need to be shown a picture to find his mate," she said quietly. "That is why I had you hold back from orgasm for six months. Those sages and mystics who practiced semen retention were not impotent men who did not desire women.

They understood the power of self-mastery, how it connects a man with the universe's wisdom even as it connects him with the deepest instincts of his own body, the animal-like sixth sense that enables a beast to find his match, his mate, the one most suitable to carry his seed." Zareena blinked now, turning away and towards the dark window as the street lights of Tulsa whipped by. "And now it is done, and you need to clear your head." She turned back to him, face calm and composed. "I suggest Las Vegas," she said without missing a beat, like she had planned it already. "I believe you know your way around the private circles in the city of . . . of clarity."

The Sheikh grunted as he turned to his window and stared out. Then he nodded. "I will drop you off at the hotel and then go directly to the airport. Call and have them file a flight plan for the jet."

"Already done," Zareena said quickly. "And the car will drop you off first. I do not mind the ride to the airport. I will do some Oklahoma sight-seeing from the window."

The Sheikh grunted again, reaching for the large silver cup of tea that had been prepared and left on the table by his seat.

"Yes," he said as the sweet tea shocked him awake, that sharpness returning as his eyes went wide. "Some clarity would be good. Channel away some of this energy that your mystics and sages were able to direct with better care. I do not pretend to be a master of my needs to such extremes. Six months was enough to almost break me, clearly. You are correct, my Sheikha. This will bring some clarity. Perhaps some relief."

8

But Zareena was the one most relieved as she watched the Sheikh lean back and sip his tea while the black limousine cruised through the Tulsa streets, gliding onto the open highway and speeding up now as the queen turned back to her window.

Yes, relieved. Relieved that Dhom did not seem to realize that not only had Zareena not told him how to find Grace Garner in that crowded room, but the Sheikh had never even asked.

Ya Allah, Dhom had never even asked.

9

"**D**id you ask me something?"

"No," said Gracie, quickly walking past the pharmacy window and fumbling for the handle of the glass-doored cooler set off to that side of the store. She reached in and grabbed a bottle of something. Iced tea, it looked like. "I was just talking to myself."

"I do that all the time," said the bespectacled pharmacist with the clean-shaved head and white coat. He smiled up from the table where he had been sitting, back from the pharmacy counter, reading a newspaper of all things. "That's why I like to hold a newspaper or a phone in front of me when it's slow. That way people think I'm just reading aloud, instead of some crazy guy who stares into space and mumbles to aliens."

"Or some crazy chick who comes all the way down here to buy that pill and then wimps out and instead reaches for this awful-tasting iced-tea," Gracie muttered as she took a swig of the nasty green stuff that desperately needed sugar to make it palatable.

She smiled at the man and walked away, realizing now that she couldn't go back there and ask for the pill. Not now that she had spoken to the man and he had seen her face so clearly! This wasn't her neighborhood store—it was a pharmacy inside the giant supermarket in the suburbs of Tulsa—but still, what if this guy had a niece or nephew in her school, and what if that kid someday showed him a picture of "Gracie the Ruler," and what if that day happened tomorrow or next week? Then all the kids would know, and they were just ten years old but for sure they'd take that wooden ruler down and put up a pair of ripped panties on the wall, "Gracie the Slut" scrawled across it in whore-red lipstick.

Gracie almost spat iced-tea into an old man's cart as she laughed at her own paranoia. Yeah, she cared about her reputation. Yes, she *was* a role model to the young girls in her class, and it would *absolutely* be mortifying if everyone at school—staff included—knew what she'd done behind the curtains on

Saturday night, pushed up against the wall. But that wasn't the reason she had walked past the pharmacy counter and was now sipping this disgusting green tea. Nope. Gracie had known she wasn't going to buy that damned morning-after pill. She just wasn't going to do it. She couldn't. It was like a sickness rose up in her if she even *thought* about it, a sickness that only subsided when she told herself she wouldn't do it. It was like her body was rejecting the suggestion at a fundamental, visceral, primal level. Straight-up physical communication. Like the body had overruled the brain. Logic and common sense versus instinct and hunches. Guess what wins?

Gracie tossed the half-drunk bottle into the recycling as she strode out of the store, opening up her hair and letting the afternoon breeze have at it. God, she felt great suddenly, didn't she? Shockingly great, considering the roller coaster of elation and despair last night, that magnificent high of the most exciting, mind-blowing sex she could imagine followed by facing the sickening fear that all he wanted from her was . . .

Actually, what did he want, she asked herself for the millionth time as she touched her round belly unconsciously and squinted as she wondered where the hell she had parked her little red Honda. After all, there had clearly been a connection between them. A spark. A tingle that reminded her of high-school love, so fresh and exciting, so overwhelming and exciting. And then they were flirting, weren't they? Yes. Hell, yes. They were most *certainly* flirting, and he was most *certainly* hitting on her in a way that seemed like he wanted more than just—

But what did *you* want, she forced herself to ask now as she tightened her jaw and reminded herself of what she always tried to convey to the older girls in school when discussions about boys came up. It's about what *you* want. If you don't want to go out with him, then don't do it. Doesn't matter if he gets annoyed. All the more reason not to go out with him! What do *you* want? That's the only question that matters to the strong, confident, feminist of today's America.

And what *did* I want, Gracie wondered as she finally saw her Honda hatchback cowering behind a mammoth black truck. Did I want more than just sex? Sure. Of course. That's what any woman wants, yes? That's the dream, isn't it? A boyfriend, a fiancé, a husband. A courtship, an engagement, a wedding. A baby.

Now that sickening emptiness roared in suddenly, hitting her like a gut-punch, making her seize up as she reached her car. She slammed her palms down on the back glass of the hatchback, telling herself to grow the hell up, that she was an adult woman in post-feminist America, that she had indulged in a night of wild sex, that the man hadn't promised her anything, hadn't said he would call her the next day, hadn't said much more than his name and how he was going to "kidnap her for the evening."

She laughed as she thought back to those old stories of Arabian kings kidnapping white women and forcing them to bear half-breed children who would rise to inherit desert kingdoms, lead armies into battle, hold court with the commoners, continue royal bloodlines, blah blah blah, yak yak yak. Madness. Silliness. Nonsense. But funny, yeah? And God, he did say he was *Sheikh* Dhomaar, yeah? How do you spell that, anyway? Dough-mar? Doh-more?

Now after spending the previous night refusing to let herself do it, Gracie finally pulled out her phone and searched for his name, trying all kinds of variations on the spelling, ignoring the feeling that it was lame and stalkerish. After all, if a guy did that it would be *totally* psycho-stalker stuff, right?

She smiled as she ran her fingers through her hair, steeling herself for what she knew had to be the truth. But still her smile tightened when she saw his photograph pop up. And slowly the smile faded. Slowly the steely resolve wavered. And finally the phone was tossed into the front seat as Gracie fought back tears that were not of disappointment but of anger. Contempt. Not for him, but for herself. Rage directed inwards. Contempt for her own lameness to even *start* to believe that this guy could have been the real thing, that she could really meet an exciting, charismatic, handsome man in a crowded room, melt under his confident advances, flutter her eyelids at his smooth Arabian accent, clench her fat butt when he touched her without asking, spread her chubby thighs for him when he pushed his hardness between her legs before she could even pronounce his goddamn name.

And she must have known the truth the moment she saw him, yes? She must have known it, and she let him have her anyway, Gracie thought as she angrily grabbed her phone and tapped the screen to close the photograph that looked like it had been taken for Vogue magazine.

She missed with her trembling finger and tapped it again. But now instead of closing the browser she zoomed in on the photograph, and she was forced to confront her own stupidity and gooey-eyed lameness when she saw the close up of Sheikh Dhomaar of Mizra on a red carpet with his wife, the slim, elegant, hijab-clad Queen Zareena.

10

Queen Zareena folded the smooth black satin of her hijab before placing it on the wooden dresser of the hotel suite for Alma her attendant to put away in the morning.

By now Grace Garner would know that Dhom is married and so it was nothing more than one night of indulgence, Zareena thought, smiling as she stood up straight, all alone in just her beige panties. She hadn't worn a bra—a habit from her teenage years, when it was the only form of rebellion she could get away with as far as her clothing choices went. Of course, now the habit of wearing the traditional hijab was ingrained in her and she loved that she didn't need to worry about what to wear. She had stuck with the no-bra habit as well—though now it wasn't an act of secret rebellion as much as it simply felt more comfortable. Granted, she had the chest-proportions of an eleven-year-old girl, which made it a bit easier, she thought with a sigh as she pinched her tight brown nipples and allowed a thin smile to break.

Not like the magnificent curves of that American schoolteacher, Zareena thought as she tried to shut down the images she had seen of Gracie Garner over the past six months. Those large, wide hips. Beautiful round buttocks. Heavy breasts that made Zareena fantasize about what Grace's nipples would look like, feel like, taste like . . .

Enough, the queen told herself as she felt a gentle wetness seep into those beige cotton panties. You have fantasized about this woman enough, and now it is your turn to show some self-mastery. Already Alma complains that you close your eyes and drift into your own mind too much when she is with you in the darkness. It is not fair to Alma. You must respect her loyalty and sacrifice. Yes, she is bound to serve her queen like any of the palace attendants, but she keeps the queen's secrets in a way none other could.

Perhaps one last time, Zareena thought now as she heard Alma quietly step into the master bedroom of the suite, standing at the door behind Zareena, waiting to be summoned to the bed. One last fantasy with Grace Garner, a woman I have never met, a woman who will be carrying my soon-to-be-adopted child, Mizra's future ruler. Yes, one more time I can have her in my fantasy. After all, my husband had the pleasure of having her in the flesh. And we both deserve the indulgence, do we not? We have both paid the price for keeping that side of our lives secret, for committing to keep the needs of our flesh private forever, behind closed doors, behind thick curtains, behind the veil of our sexless marriage.

Yes, we have both paid the price, my dear Dhom, Zareena thought as she felt herself clench inside those panties as she smelled Alma's need in the dry air-conditioned air of the room.

Zareena turned now, pointing at the bed as Alma's gaunt brown face lit up at being summoned by her queen, her consort, her lover, her goddess. And as Alma crawled onto the bed and stuck her slim bottom up the air, Zareena smiled and reached for the camel-hide whip that she always carried with her personal effects.

Ya Allah, she thought as she stroked Alma's smooth brown skin with the rough tassels of the rawhide whip. We have both paid the price of secrecy in the way our private needs have escalated over the years, the way our fantasies have expanded as we got older, got bolder. And now both Dhom and I are twisted and turned, bruised and burned, our needs only suitable for the most private of stages, the most willing of partners.

We have paid the price, she thought one last time before raising her arm and bringing the whip down with *blinding* speed, striking the first lash as Alma screamed under the yellow light.

And soon Alma cried out again, again and again as the queen whipped her raw, whipped her ripe, whipped her red. Then finally, with a feminine growl Zareena tossed the whip aside, pushed Alma onto her back, and straddled her face as she pulled those beige panties aside. Now the queen closed her eyes, allowed her mind to wander. Soon she was grinding ferociously on Alma's face, rubbing and moaning, finally smiling as she felt Alma's long, stiff tongue slide into her.

And as the queen's eyes fluttered and closed, she allowed the image of that American woman to float in, those creamy white breasts, wonderfully heavy thighs, magnificent buttocks, pretty round face twisted in a grimace of ecstasy at the hands of Queen Zareena. And those unseen, oft-imagined nipples.

"Yes, you can have me," Grace whispered in Zareena's dream as the queen wailed her way to the first climax of what promised to be a long evening for Alma. "You can taste me, suck me, savor me. You can have me."

11

"You can have me too if you like, great Sheikh," whispered the red-leather-clad madam of the private club that might as well have had Dhom's name on a golden plaque near the soundproofed rooms of its spacious basement. "The girls have missed you. But not as much as I, my Lord."

She bowed her head and glanced up at the Sheikh as he stood before her in the lavish, leather-and-velvet outfitted reception area of the underground club. Dhom knew this woman well—indeed, he knew every inch of her, inside and outside, every nook and cranny, every crack and crevasse. Of course, much of that was from when both he and she were younger—though he still dragged her into his padded playroom once in a while to give her a taste of those younger days, perhaps to remind her that his needs had escalated beyond the point of what her aging body could safely handle.

"This is not the time for you," Dhom said as he forced a smile and glanced around the empty club, which had been cleared at a moment's notice when Dhom called to say he would be arriving. Indeed, amongst the high-rollers that might have protested at being denied entry, none came close to how high the Sheikh rolled, how *hard* the Sheikh rolled. "Today my needs are too great for you, my tender mistress of the night. I fear I will break you."

"Oh, Dhom, you know how I crave to be broken by you again," she cooed as she strolled out from behind her smooth black desk and sauntered over to where the Sheikh stood a few feet away.

She wore a red leather bodysuit, low-cut with a push-up black corset, black fishnet hugging her thighs that had once been a lot fuller. She looked thin and frail, the Sheikh thought as he smiled and obliged her with a rough nipple-pinch as she undid the drawstring of her corset and offered him her bare breasts.

His cock moved as the woman gasped and tried to reach for his erection. But he grabbed her hand and pushed her away. She stumbled in her heels, and the

Surrogate for the Sheikh

Sheikh quickly reached out and caught her so she wouldn't fall. Ya Allah, he needed to be careful today! Too much energy that he could not understand, let alone control!

All that talk about pair bonding and the male instinct to protect the female—especially the female carrying his seed. By God, if Zareena's "hunch" was correct, then this American woman would conceive from their encounter that night! Perhaps the conception had already occurred! His seed already taking its place in her fertile womb!

That is what Zareena believes, yes? he thought. That my incomprehensible need to be with Grace, to go to this woman I do not know, to have her again, take her again, love her again, claim her again, keep her safe, let her know she is mine to protect . . . all of it is the wisdom of instinct? Instinct that is further enhanced by a subconscious knowledge that she will indeed bear my child? This feeling of being drawn to Grace is just that? Dumb instinct? Or is it divine wisdom? Are they the same? Yah, Allah, Zareena had turned me inside out with her babble!

Dhomaar exhaled and waited until the madam had regained her balance and tucked away her turgid, silicone-enhanced boobs before he turned and slowly walked along the perimeter of the anteroom. Along the black-painted walls were closed doors, each of them leading to a different setup, a different woman, a different fantasy. Behind this door lay silver chains and golden handcuffs. This next room had a replica of the medieval rack. A third room contained expertly fashioned wooden stocks, where the Sheikh knew a woman was already imprisoned, her head and arms locked in smooth wood, buttocks sticking up, legs spread in helpless submission.

Dhom had always had a fascination for the imprisoned woman, a woman bound and waiting, in a cell or dungeon, at his mercy, at his disposal. It was sick, he knew. Twisted, he acknowledged. Perhaps it was a natural reaction to the bonds which duty and responsibility had placed upon his own hands, his own body, his own life. Perhaps because he had sacrificed a normal marriage and sex-life to satisfy the medieval laws of his kingdom, he felt this sick need to fantasize about *being* that medieval Arab Sheikh, with white women imprisoned in his dungeons, tied and spread, proud western women ready to be tamed into submission, taught a lesson!

Taught a lesson, he repeated in his head as he smirked at the memory of telling Grace Garner the schoolteacher that he too was a teacher! What would he have said if she had asked what his specialty was? Would he have told her the truth? Told her his fantasy? Told her how he taught women to step into his private fantasy? To make it their own fantasy? To learn to enjoy being helpless and bound in the great medieval king's dungeons?

And now his mind whipped back to the memory of Grace in his arms last night, his body hardening, his green eyes glazing over as his cock pushed against the front of his trousers. Dhomaar glanced at the madam, who was making no secret of where she was looking, licking her lips at the grotesquely awesome peak in the Sheikh's trousers.

The Sheikh turned away from her, slowly running his hand along the black-painted wall as he walked the perimeter of the room. "I cannot," he muttered as he lowered his arm and clenched his fist. "I cannot follow this plan of ours, Zareena. I am sorry. The urge is too strong. The need is too great. Perhaps I am risking everything, but I am not a mystic who can find the beauty in denying his need. I am not a sage who can laugh as he turns away from what his body wants." His jaw went tight now, green eyes still glazed over but attaining a strange focus—perhaps the same sort of otherworldly focus that had been in operation in that crowded ballroom, the trance-like focus that had drawn the Sheikh to this curvy schoolteacher in her red dress even though he did not know her at all, did not know beforehand what she looked like but somehow already knew what she ... smelled like, tasted like, *felt* like?!

Ya Allah, he thought now as he turned absent-mindedly and stared at the frowning madam without really seeing her. By God, not only was I drawn to Grace when I saw her, but I was perhaps drawn to her *before* I saw her, was I not? Because not only did Zareena not tell me how to find her in a crowd, but I never even thought to *ask* Zareena! And so could it be . . . could it be that I already *knew*?!

I already knew, the Sheikh thought as his body firmed up and a startling sense of clarity took over. Ya Allah, I already *knew*!

And now exhilaration *roared* through the Sheikh as he grinned like a madman and *ran* towards the dark stairs leading back up to the light. "Bill me for all the women, and then double it," he called to the bewildered, frowning madam as he took the stairs two at a time, whipping out his phone and informing his men to wake up the co-pilot and force-feed him some coffee.

By God, this is real, he thought as he strode to his limo and got in. Perhaps this semen retention thing has indeed turned me into a mystic, taken me to enlightenment!

"Clarity indeed," he muttered as he watched the neon-lit streets of downtown Las Vegas whip by as the limo headed for the airport. "I am learning something about myself."

He grinned again as he wondered if Grace would be expecting him or not, whether she would turn him away or receive him, if she would open up for him again or shut him down after his perfectly executed disappearing act last night. A disappearing act which was the *only* thing which was an act! Everything else was *real*, by God!

"*Ana sawf mmil' lakum,*" he muttered finally as the airport pulled into view. Now his smile changed form, his cock pushing to full-mast in his trousers as the realization of what he was going to do sunk in. "Have you also reached this enlightenment, my curvy teacher from Tulsa?" he said out loud. "No matter. I will take you there if you have not. I will take you there again and again. Again and forever." He looked at his platinum watch with the thirteen recessed diamonds, seeing the reflection of his own green eyes sparkling in its face. "Sunday already. Well, Ms. Grace Garner. I suppose it will have to be Sunday school."

12

"Sunday afternoon, and I'm in school," Gracie muttered as she unlocked the large green door of the staff room on the third floor of Wilson Park Middle School in south Tulsa.

The main doors to the building had been open, like they were every weekend: the school had a great athletic program, and there were always optional coaching sessions for the teams on Saturdays and Sundays. Today looked like girls' soccer and boys' basketball, judging from the voices she could hear and where the cars had been parked in the lot. Some parents were here as well, it seemed, and Gracie had smiled as she caught a glimpse of a few over-enthusiastic moms and dads giving advice on the soccer field, much to the coach's patient annoyance.

But the staff room was empty, and Gracie sighed as she went to her desk at the far end of the large open room. She had snagged a great spot in the back, right near the café area, and over the past year had slowly pushed her heavy desk closer and closer to the window along the nearest wall until she had quietly and surreptitiously taken over that window and its view of the front lawn and parking lots.

"Gracie the Ruler extends her empire," Ms. Walters the principal had declared when she finally noticed how Gracie's desk was now pushed up flush against the window, blocking anyone else from standing there. "An invasion under the cover of smiles and sweetness."

Gracie had grimaced and forced an embarrassed smile when she caught the few other teachers glancing up from their desks, looks of vague satisfaction on most of their faces, like they had noticed but had been too polite to say anything—to her, at least.

"OK, who's the undercover agent who ratted me out?" Gracie said loudly, drawing laughs and a few embarrassed smiles from her colleagues. "Come on. You know how Gracie the Ruler deals with spies, enemies of the state."

"I am the State, I should remind you," Ms. Walters

had said in a mock-angry tone, crossing her arms over her chest as a few more chuckles rose up from the other teachers, some jovial whoops and playful applause, cries of *Go to War* and *Have it Out* and even a *Who's your Mama* from the peanut gallery.

Of course, everyone loved Gracie, and every kingdom bends the rules for rulers they love, and so Ms. Walters had waved her off when Gracie stood and turned her big bottom to the room and made a huge show of trying to move the heavy desk back away from the window. The staff had cheered and clapped as Ms. Walters backed down, and so now Gracie owned that spot. Might is right! The invasion had been successful! Queen Gracie rules again!

She exhaled hard as she tossed her bag into the empty plastic chair against the wall. Then she sighed and sank into her swivel chair with the battered red cushion. She didn't feel in charge right now, she thought as she put her elbows on her desk and rested her chin in her hands and frumped and pouted, blowing out through closed lips like a sulky child.

"Well, at least you've learned something," she said out loud as she watched the girls on the soccer field, where the coach had finally sent the parents to the sidelines. "You've learned what every girl with a double-chin and a fat ass already knows: That if a handsome stranger with the body of an underwear model and the bank account of an oil baron wants you,

Surrogate for the Sheikh

it sure as hell isn't because he wants you to bear his children."

The guy was probably snipped, Gracie thought as she tried again to rationalize why she hadn't taken the plan-B pill that morning. *That's why he came inside me without a second thought. That made sense, didn't it?* After all, when she plucked up the fortitude to scan through the few non-Arabic articles about Sheikh Dhomaar and Queen Zareena, there was no mention of them having any kids. Strange, but whatever. Maybe they had decided not to have kids. Maybe the queen couldn't conceive. Either way, perhaps Dhomaar had decided to get a vasectomy as a "risk management" procedure. After all, a billionaire king from a conservative Islamic kingdom probably didn't want to take the chance of one of his escapades turning into eighteen years of child support and perhaps a very expensive, very public divorce.

Though as a king and queen, don't they need *an heir to continue their royal bloodline or whatever,* Grace wondered as she absentmindedly watched a black limo stop at a traffic light a few blocks down the street. *Isn't that how royalty and kingdoms work? Or is that just in the old world? Maybe just in old England and Germany or whatever. Who knew how Sheikhs and Sheikdoms operated.*

Perhaps you should bother to learn about Sheikhs and Sheikhdoms, the thought came as Gracie frowned at the sight of that black limousine slowly taking a left turn and winding its way down the driveway leading to the horseshoe-roundabout of the front entrance to Wilson Park Middle School.

And as that thought about Sheikhs and kings, learning and lessons, teaching and being taught swirled through Gracie's rapidly spinning mind, she felt her body seize up with that sickening fear, that dizzying excitement, that spiraling exhilaration that came *screaming* in like an invading army.

"No way," she muttered as she stood from her chair and leaned across her desk so she could see what was happening. The limo had stopped, and two men in black suits and sunglasses had stepped out from the front doors and were briskly walking around to the large rear doors.

"Oh, my lord," she gasped when she saw him, the Sheikh himself, that towering beast of a man. He stepped out onto the paving and stretched himself like even the limo had been cramped. Tailored black suit, white shirt, no tie, no pretense, all business. All business, and all *man*!

Even from three floors up his heft and presence sent a blast of electricity through her so quick she almost swooned as she absentmindedly crawled onto the desk, her brown eyes wide, face draining of color before rapidly going red as she gasped again and then crawled back away from the window when the Sheikh stood there with his hands on his hips, looking up,

Surrogate for the Sheikh

scanning the windows of the school as if searching for her, his gaze moving up to her window astonishingly fast, like he knew where to look.

Of course, he couldn't know where to look. How could he even know she'd be at school on a Sunday? More spies, Gracie wondered in an almost manic state of disbelief and excitement as she stepped back away from the window, not sure if the Sheikh had seen her fat face staring down at him!

Now she *ran* to the staff bathroom, frantically clawing at her hair, the long brown tresses hopelessly ravaged by the afternoon breeze in that pharmacy parking lot from earlier that day. Shit. No hairbrush. No makeup. Tightish v-neck white t-shirt that showed nice cleavage but made her look like the Pillsbury doughboy around her stomach. And mom jeans. *Mom jeans*!

"When will you learn to take all those silly chick-magazine's advice and dress every day like you're going to run into your ex, you stupid *cow*!" Gracie shouted at her reflection before walking out into the staff room and wondering if hell, should she meet him or hide? He had glanced up at her window just as she ducked back. But had he seen her? Maybe he saw movement at the window; but no way he could tell it was her, right? It was hard to see inside the school during the day, with the sky and clouds reflecting off the slightly coated windows.

Dress every day like you're going to run into your

ex, she told herself again, deciding there was no way she could let him see her like this, that after seeing her all radiant and red in the grand ballroom he'd only be disappointed, perhaps even disgusted!

"That's bad advice," she said out loud as she spun around in the empty room wondering if she should hide in the bathroom or in one of the classrooms. "What those magazines *should* say is to dress every day like you're going to meet a billionaire Sheikh with whom you had wild, wonderful sex last night and who for some reason has tracked you down a day later to see if you're still the alluring American woman in that red dress and heels, black panties and lipstick, perfect hair and flawless skin.

She stood there frozen and hyperventilating for what seemed like a long time, her eyes closed tight as she listened for the sound of that squeaky metal elevator arriving on her floor. She held her breath as she listened for the click of his Italian leather shoes on the ugly blue tiles of the hallway. But nothing. Silence.

That feeling of despair began to tug at the corners of Gracie's paranoia now, and she suddenly felt that emptiness from last night rush back in, a sick feeling that yet again he wasn't going to show up, that he had come all the way here and changed his mind at the last minute. Perhaps he did see her face in the window, and perhaps he was disgusted at the sight of her without makeup, her hair all mussed. Maybe the reflective coating on those damn government-issued windows made her face look all blurry and ugly, and it repulsed him. Or maybe he wasn't even here for her! Maybe he was fucking one of those single moms on the soccer field! Those whores! Those sluts! That bastard! Ohmygod, how did I suddenly turn into a *psycho*?!

She swallowed hard and then willed herself to take a step to the window. It had been long enough that he'd be up here by now. She looked, and sure enough, there was that long black limo still parked in the horseshoe roundabout. Still here. He hadn't disappeared. He was real. He was here. And he was here for her.

Now slowly her natural confidence began to assert itself. She thought back to how aroused the Sheikh had been last night. She thought about how he had grasped her hips like he couldn't stop himself, squeezed her bottom like he loved it, sucked her boobs like he wanted to devour her. And the way he came . . . oh, *God*, the way he came! Like a geyser blasting to the surface! An undersea volcano exploding in the depths of her ocean! That wasn't just because of her makeup and her hair! That arousal was deeper, stronger, harder.

Harder, she thought again, her own arousal ratcheting up as the memory of being pushed against the wall came back with such vividness that she had to lean on her desk as a dizziness rushed in. She could feel her pussy tighten, her clit stiffen, her panties moisten with fresh wetness, a new yearning, as if it was anticipating something, anticipating some*one*, anticipating *him*.

Stop it, she thought as she stepped all the way to the window and boldly pulled the bottom pane up, deciding right then and there to send him back to his goddamn island. If he's here, then he's only here for one thing. He's a married man from another country and he thinks he's got an easy booty call. Sure, maybe I gave him reason to think that, the way I swooned and giggled and spread like a slut for him. But that was last night and this is today. I don't know *who* that woman in the red dress was last night, but this is *my* turf now, and I decide what happens in my realm.

She snorted now as she leaned on the window sill and squinted down at the men in black suits and sunglasses. God, for a moment had she actually considered giving him what he no doubt was here for! In school? She was willing to risk getting fired, being pretty much blacklisted from every public teaching job in the state, if not the country? And for what? For this guy, who wasn't even that . . . wait, where was he?

Now she saw him again. He stood alone in the middle of the manicured front lawn, right next to the sign that said "Stay on the Path." He was on the phone, nodding, gesturing, clenching his fist, speaking loudly in Arabic, gesturing again.

And then, without warning, the Sheikh *smashed* the phone into the pavement, kicking away the debris as one of his bodyguards hurriedly cleared up the mess, being careful to stay out of the Sheikh's way.

"Ya Allah, Zareena!" he roared into the air, and she could hear him clearly—shit, they could hear him on the soccer field too, it seemed; though they couldn't see him.

Zareena? So his wife knows?! Did she just find out? And now he's in deep shit? Who the hell knows. Either way, time to close this window and step back, Gracie, she told herself. Step away from the fire. Turn and walk away.

13

"Turn and walk away, Dhomaar," Zareena had said into the phone. "You are lucky Habib's people saw you drive up to the school in your big black car and thought to call me. If I had not been warned, with one thrust of your royal cock you would have undone six months of work. Perhaps undone a hundred years of work!"

"I do not see the problem," the Sheikh had growled into the phone as he paced the driveway outside the school, finally stepping onto the off-limits grass and mentally cursing himself for even answering the goddamn phone. "So it will be two times instead of just once. Perhaps it is better to make sure."

Surrogate for the Sheikh

"I am *already* sure," Zareena screamed, her voice so piercing that the Sheikh had to pull the phone back from his ear. "And if you go to her again, it could change everything! Do you not see, you goddamn beast? Do you not see I am trying to stop your animal instincts from leading us to disaster?"

"No, I do not see anything," Dhomaar muttered, looking up at the school building and catching some movement at the far window of the third floor. "I do not see how just one more time will lead us to this *disaster* you speak of!"

"Oh, Dhomaar, my Sheikh, my king, my partner," Zareena had rasped in an urgent whisper. "Oh, Dhom, I know you have denied that part of you for so long. I know you have denied yourself a deep connection with a woman and instead loyally served your kingdom and your people. I know you feel a connection with this woman—that was the entire *point* of this elaborate scheme! For you to conceive a child with innocent spontaneity, to let your need build up and then put you in a room with a fertile, vivacious woman who is peaking in her cycle. But do you not see how even that is a mirage? That we have knowingly and consciously manipulated your instincts and emotions to achieve our purpose? A purpose that will be greatly complicated if you give this woman reason to believe you might want more than just one night of release, that the encounter meant something."

The Sheikh had stayed quiet as he turned away

from that window. He grimaced as he listened. They had discussed this earlier, he knew. The most delicate part of this plan would not be the seduction itself but the nine months that followed. After all, this woman was a surrogate but she did not know it! There was no legal agreement. It was a deception. An illusion. A mirage. The only thing genuine was the sex!

"Dhomaar," Zareena had said. "Think about what you will be doing to her if you see her again. You cannot marry her. And so if you give her reason to believe you care for her, then . . . then . . ."

"Then she may be so angry, hurt, indignant at the deception that she may never agree to give up custody when the time comes to lay the cards on the table," the Sheikh said, nodding. "I know, Zareena. We have discussed it. I accepted your word for it, but one thing always bothered me: What makes you think she would give up custody anyway? What woman gives up her child? If she believes it was just a one-night stand, then she will sue me for child support and that will be it! I may not even be allowed visitation!"

"I told you I have it worked out," Zareena snapped. "She will give up the child. Trust me. I know what I am doing, Dhom."

"Do you?" the Sheikh growled into the phone, squeezing the little handset so hard he could feel the metal bend in protest. "Then tell me your plan. Right now, Zareena. Even secrecy has its limits, and I am at that limit. Speak now, my queen. I command you, dammit!"

Zareena had paused, and Dhom could hear her take a long breath and hold it. A strange uneasiness rose up in him as he waited for her to speak. When she did, her voice was calm, controlled . . . contrived?

"The plan is straightforward, Dhom," she said quickly as she exhaled. "I told you we sought out women who were alone, in low paying jobs, no family money, not even any real family to lean on. This woman fits all those criteria. So now I have instructed Habib to wait until we know she is pregnant—more importantly, until *she* knows she is pregnant—and then to engineer a . . . a crisis, let us say."

"Crisis? What in bloody hell does that mean, Zareena? Ya Allah, my Sheikha! I trust you more than I trust myself, but perhaps I have allowed you to keep me in the dark for too much of this. After all, it is I who is accountable to this woman! It is I—"

"You are not accountable to anyone other than your nation and your duty!" Zareena roared into the phone like a lioness at dawn. "Do not forget why we are doing this! Do not forget why—"

"Remind me again, because I am having a hard time," the Sheikh shouted back in rapid-fire Arabic. "Because the oases are turning to salt? And a blind old Sheikh is whispering to himself about ending our line and invading our island kingdom? That is it, correct? Ya Allah, it sounds bloody mad as I say it!"

"That is why you must leave it to me," Zareena said. "Like you said, you must trust me more than you trust yourself right now. Because Dhom, you *cannot* trust yourself right now. Your judgment is deeply compromised . . . compromised because you are operating at a severe disadvantage, my great Sheikh."

"Yes? And what is that disadvantage, Zareena?"

"Your royal cock," Zareena spat into the phone. "And your heavy, swinging balls. Now if there is even one part of you that has not submitted to your arousal right now, then get back into that bloody car and walk away from this. Walk away from her. I never expected you to fully understand or even agree with me. I only expected you to remain true to your sense of duty, and to have faith that in the end I want nothing more than what is best for my nation. Now I am done talking. It is your decision. You are your own man, even though right now you are owned by your arousal. I just hope you can be damned sure that when the arousal is satisfied, you will not find yourself—"

And Dhom had *smashed* the phone into the hard paving before she finished, *kicking* at the debris, *slamming* his fists down onto the hood of the limo as he shouted *Zareena!* in anger.

Then he caught sight of Grace from the corner of his eye. There she was, leaning out of the open window, like Rapunzel in her tower, looking down at her prince. And suddenly he was calm, like her presence made everything all right, made everything make sense.

He watched as she darted away from the window,

and he waited for her to come back. But she did not, and the Sheikh sighed and walked to the open back door of the car, leaning on the door and frowning as he rubbed his stubble.

A crisis, he thought now as he went over Zareena's words. What was she planning? Something to get Grace fired, perhaps? Remove her source of income? Make her panic when she realizes she is pregnant and does not have a job? Yes, of course Grace would reach out for child support, if not more. So perhaps Zareena hopes this "crisis" would make a custody case easier? An unemployed single mother with no real savings on one side, a billionaire king with a wife willing to accept the child on the other side? The cultural differences might still swing the case in Grace's favor, but perhaps Zareena was counting on settling this out of court once Grace was in a financial crisis? Wasn't one of the so-called criteria that the woman would be selfless, would put the child's welfare over her own if things got "complicated?" Would Zareena play on Grace's selfless maternal instincts to make her choose what would be best for the child, even if it meant giving up custody? Was Zareena capable of it? Was *Gracie* capable of it? Who knew. Who the *hell* knew!

Yes, who the bloody hell knows, and in fact who the bloody hell *cares*! Yes, who *cares*, he thought now as he stepped away from the car and stared up at that window. Here I am, a goddamn *King*, going in circles trying to understand the motives and machinations of a woman? Of *two* women? Who gives a *damn*!? I am the *king*, goddamn it! I am a *man*, goddamn it! Women may play the game with manipulation and secrecy, with influence and persuasion, worrying about signs from the universe and messages from the angels. But the only messages I care about come from my goddamn *balls*! The only sign that matters is the way my *cock* hardens when I think of that woman and her curves! Her breasts and buttocks. Her lips and eyes. Her crack and her beautiful, magnificent *cunt*!

With a *roar* of laughter he made his decision, and now it was done. The king was a king again, master of his domain, alpha of his jungle. And the king was going to take his queen. The master was going to claim his slave. The beast was going to ravish his mate.

14

"Get away from me, you *beast*," she said as she fought him off, giggling and protecting her bouncing breasts that were already raw from the way he had pinched them just a moment ago, right in the middle of the empty staff room. "*Away!* Are you *mad*? This is my *workplace*! If someone sees us . . ." Grace cried as she backed up against her desk while the Sheikh lunged for her again, grinning like a madman, those green eyes glazed with the fire of his need. "And we're *not* going to do anything until we talk. We need to *talk*, Dhomaar!"

"We need to talk, Dhomaar," Grace had said stoically just a few minutes earlier as she ran her fingers through her hair and looked up at the towering Sheikh who had come bursting in through the staff room's green doors, those green eyes ablaze, lush red lips twisted in a manic smile, the black of his tailored suit looking deep and rich, his thick hair dark and wavy. "I'm not a part of your world. And you sure as hell aren't a part of mine. We shared a fun night, and that's all it was. I don't blame you. You didn't misrepresent yourself. I mean, not really. I mean, I think we—"

But the Sheikh just waved off her serious, sophisticated, articulate, sensible *babble* with a grunt. Then he grabbed her by the wrists and tried to kiss her immediately, as if he had the right to do it. Of course she had pushed him away, folding her arms over her breasts even as she tried to stay calm, tried to pull back her own arousal, tried to hide away the fact that she was . . . was *elated* to see him come up there. It meant something that he was here, didn't it? If nothing more than an ego boost! After all, the guy was married. To a queen. A queen who probably knew about Gracie, judging from that phone-smashing scene outside. And still he had come. For another taste of American pie? A farewell fuck before he went back to his wife and country?

But that's all it is—a nice ego boost, she had told herself as she tried not to smile at his cocky, playful advances, the way this towering Sheikh was grinning like a horny schoolboy as he tried to kiss her again, tried to grab her by the waist and pull her into his hard body. So he was here and he wanted her. Great. There's one for the water-cooler on Monday! How was your weekend, Gracie? Ah, nothing special. Fucked a super-hot Sheikh behind the curtains in a crowded ballroom. Then he followed me to school and tried to kiss me. But I said no. Sent him back to his wife, the Queen of their island kingdom in the Gulf of Oman. Seemed like the right thing to do. I'm not a home-wrecker. I'm not that kinda gal. One taste and off you go, Mister! My fat thighs don't spread twice for the same Sheikh! Woo hoo!

So she pushed him back and shook her head and covered her body and tried to look as stern as possible. She was a teacher, goddamn it. She could look stern, right?! God, he was so hot. God, he was so hard. God, she wanted to just sit up on her big desk and let him—

"I'm not a part of your world, and you're not a part of mine," she said again, her voice coming across good and stern even though she wasn't sure what the hell the words meant. But she kept talking. Just keep talking, she told herself—just like she had told herself last night in the ballroom when it became clear that the *last* thing this man with a raging erection for her wanted was to sit and *chat*!

But she opened her fat mouth and started to speak

even as the arousal flowed through her in the most alarming way. Still she talked, scolding him for not showing up at the table last night, lambasting him for being married and doing what he did, guilt-tripping him for putting her in a position where she might be destroying some other woman's marriage. She thought she was going mad as she stood there and heard herself speak, for a moment realizing she was using the same tone of voice she used with her ten-year-olds!

"You really are a teacher, yes?" he said, finally stopping his advances on her boobs and standing up straight even as his cock pushed against his trousers in the most incredibly distracting way.

"Yes, and you're in my classroom, so I'm in charge," she said firmly, trying desperately not to look at the way his cock was flexing as he shamelessly glanced at the cleavage peeking out the V of that white t-shirt.

"Are you in charge? Really?" he said, stroking his chin as he slowly took a step towards her and stopped. "Well, that is interesting. Should I call you Ms. Garner? Perhaps Ma'am, like they do in England?"

She broke a half-smile. "Actually I tell the kids to call me Gracie. Though most of them call me Gracie the Ruler, thanks to—"

"Thanks to what?"

"Never mind. We have other things to talk about. More important things."

The Sheikh shrugged. "Not really. I did not come

here to talk at all, in fact," he said in the most nonchalantly shameless way as Gracie turned red and touched her bare neck.

"OK, listen, Dhomaar," she whispered as he took another step towards her, his scent reaching her now, that hint of betelnut spice, red sage, green tobacco leaf. That pungency. That heat. Oh, God. "Listen. It's not that I'm not attracted to you—"

"So you are attracted to me. I am shocked. Really. I had no clue," he growled as he gently pulled at her open hair, playing with the brown tresses as she shivered and tried to keep speaking.

"But you're married," she whispered. "You're married, and I can't do that to another woman. It's not me. It's not right. It's not—"

"It's not your concern," he whispered, that right hand snaking around to the back of her neck now, fingers slowly grasping her hair down by the roots, grip tightening as he leaned in with those dark, luscious lips. "Zareena is well aware of—"

He stopped, his breath catching, eyes breaking contact with hers for a moment. Gracie frowned as she caught the flinch in his expression, the inflection in his tone. Yes, she had guessed that his wife had found out. Or perhaps it was a don't-ask don't-tell situation like it was with a lot of weird rich people. But "well aware" sounded odd, didn't it? And this guy had a perfect command of English, so it wasn't like he misspoke.

Gracie frowned again as she looked into his eyes. If she let him kiss her now, she knew there'd be no stopping until it was done, until he was done, until she was done. And by then maybe this conversation would be done. No, she needed to harness her goddamn arousal and stay the course. Harness his arousal too, perhaps. Use that arousal. Come on, Gracie. You're still a woman. You can control him the way women have always controlled their men! Especially strong Southern women! Yee haw!

So with a slow breath she reached for him, sliding her soft hands down to where his pants were peaked at the crotch. He groaned as she touched him, shuddered as she rubbed him, stumbled as she closed her fingers around his cock and slowly began to jerk him back and forth.

"Go on," she whispered firmly as she pulled at his cock. "You were saying something about Zareena being well aware of . . . well aware of what, Dhom? Me? Go on."

"Ya Allah, come here," he growled as he pulled her by that fistful of hair, grabbed her left breast, tried desperately to kiss her as she turned her face away and slowed down her hand-motion. "Oh, bloody God," he groaned as he shuddered and straightened up, eyes rolling up in his head as Gracie unzipped him and carefully slipped her hand inside his trousers, massaging his enormous package as he groaned and rumbled.

Now with two hands she unbuckled and unbuttoned him, letting those smooth black trousers slide down past his muscular hips. She gasped when she smelled the warm, clean musk of his crotch, and with trembling fingers she pulled the waistband of his dark blue silk underwear down over his massive bulge, the peak of which pressed against a large wet spot from his discharge.

His cock *sprang* out as she released him, and she almost jerked back with the shock of how hard and thick it was from so close, how swollen its big head was, how shiny and brown its long shaft looked in the hazy sunlight that streamed in through those coated windows of the staff room.

Now she firmly planted her knees on the carpet that was thankfully unworn and reasonably thick in this part of the room, and as the Sheikh groaned from above her and spread his legs, she slowly massaged his heavy balls and then carefully, calmly, opened her mouth and took him in, that beast of a cock, all the way into Gracie's mouth.

15

She sucked him deep, she sucked him hard, she sucked him long. But then she pulled back and looked up at him and asked the question again.

"Talk or I stop," she said quietly but firmly, her grip still tight on his dripping cock, his royal balls still heavy in the palm of her hand.

"Ya Allah, you witch," he muttered as he grabbed her shoulders and bucked his hips, trying to push his cock back into her tantalizingly open mouth. "You cannot do this. Suck me, Gracie. Suck me like that again. Bloody hell, you will suck me. I command it!"

"This is my kingdom, not yours, Sheikh," she whispered up at him as she turned her face and flexed her thick thighs, tightening her grip around his cock and balls until he pulled back and yielded to this woman who was on her knees before him.

"You will pay for this when you are in *my* kingdom," he muttered in anguish as he ran his fingers through her hair, touched her wet lips, caressed her face.

"So you're going to take me to your kingdom, is it?" she asked as she licked the underside of his cock and then pulled back again. "You, me, and your wife the queen? One happy family? Oh right, this is just an offer to join the Sheikh's harem. How sweet! How flattering!"

"No harem," he groaned as she licked him again, massaging his balls gently. "And Zareena is . . . she is . . . ya Allah, it is not what you think, Gracie. I swear it. I would not have come back here if I thought—" He choked on his words as she rewarded him by taking his cock back into her warm mouth, closing her lips tight and sucking fiercely before releasing him again and letting him talk. He swallowed and grinned in ecstasy before shaking his head and nodding. "If I thought . . ."

But he trailed off, the playful grin on his face fading as if he had told himself he could not play this game with her, that whatever he wasn't telling her was more important than the arousal roaring through him, that this man was being torn apart by something. Something more than just cheating on his wife, Gracie thought. In fact, Grace got the sense it wasn't that at all—that for some reason having sex with other women wasn't an issue in his marriage, that Zareena didn't care. Perhaps even encouraged it!

She looked up at the Sheikh now, and Grace thought she could see past the who-gives-a-damn grin that was back on his face. There was something behind this, something behind him, something behind *them*—behind *all* of them: the Sheikh, his wife, and her, Gracie Garner, schoolteacher and seductress.

"You thought . . ." she said as she looked up at him and slowly pulled on his cock again, jerking harder and faster, her own heat rising up as she felt him harden all the damn way now, like he was going to burst, explode, come all over her. "So think, great Sheikh," she whispered as she opened her mouth and leaned forward. "Think hard, and then you will tell me everything."

And she *descended* on his cock, taking him in *all* the way, choking and gagging as he seized her head and *rammed* into her with a groan, driving his cock halfway down her goddamn throat, it seemed. But she held on, she held him in, and she sucked and swallowed, jerking her head back and forth with fury as the towering Sheikh flexed and grunted above her, growled and thrust, pulling her hair, rubbing her shoulders, desperately reaching down the front of her shirt and clawing at her boobs as she spread her legs and went lower to keep him in her mouth.

"*Ana sawf mmil' lakum,*" he groaned as she grasped his heavy balls and gently massaged them in a circular, rhythmic motion as she slowly hummed on his swollen cock. She could feel her own wetness soaking through her goddamn mom-jeans, she thought as she tightened her lips and dragged back and forth on his throbbing erection. Her own pussy was clenching inside her wet cotton panties, like it was demanding its turn now. Soon, she told her filthy little cunt as she felt almost delirious with the back-and-forth motion of her head, her fingers cupping and massaging his balls with increasing force, the way he was pulling on her shoulders, plucking on her nipples, all the while straight-up fucking her in the mouth as he grunted and muttered in Arabic.

Soon, she thought as she felt his massive body suddenly seize up as the Sheikh muttered a guttural cry of, "Ya Allah" and *grabbed* her head with both hands, *rammed* his cock all the way deep, and *blasted* his load into her mouth, holding her head in place as she choked and then swallowed, her throat opening up for him as he poured his clean semen down into her, his balls seizing and releasing as she massaged him to completion.

He came into her mouth for almost a full minute, it seemed, and Gracie surprised herself by how she had managed to keep him inside and swallow. Not that she had a choice, she realized for a moment of fleeting alarm when she felt his strong hands slowly let go of her hair, releasing their viselike grip on her head.

Now with a drawn out groan of satisfaction the Sheikh pulled out of her mouth, his long cock slowly sliding past her wet lips, its glistening shaft throbbing as he withdrew, that thick vein on his cock pulsating from the force of his orgasm. When the swollen head of his cock emerged, Gracie gasped and drew back, falling back on her bottom in exhaustion as she propped herself up with her arms and wiped away the long trail of saliva and semen hanging down her lower lip.

The Sheikh staggered back and fell into that plastic chair, muscular brown thighs spread wide as he panted and heaved, looking down at her with amazement.

"By God, woman," he muttered. "Oh, bloody hell. You have no goddamn idea what that felt like."

"I think I have *some* idea," Gracie said in amusement as she herself panted and puffed from the exertion. She glanced into his eyes, feeling a strange warmth come over her. It wasn't just her arousal, she thought. There was a warmth from the knowledge of what she had made him feel. A satisfaction and pleasure that seemed more than just sexual. It felt almost . . . loving.

Stop it, she told herself as she imagined for a moment that she saw the same warmth in the Sheikh's green eyes, that he wasn't just looking at some random woman who had just sucked him off to a mindblowing climax—that instead he was looking at a *special* woman who had just sucked him off to a mindblowing climax!

Stop it, she told herself again as she saw him smile wide and reach for her, pulling her to her feet effortlessly without even needing to stand up off that damned chair.

"Sit," he said as he grabbed her by the waist and spun her so her bottom faced him. "Sit on the Sheikh's lap. Come."

Gracie snorted as she brushed her hair from her face. "Um, I'm pretty sure that chair can't handle our combined weight. I don't even dare sit in it alone. Seriously, those plastic legs are going to splay out, and we'll be—"

"I would like your legs to be splayed out soon," he grunted, grabbing her jeans by the waistband from behind and pushing his hand between her legs from under her ass, roughly massaging her mound from beneath as she gasped from his forceful touch. "You do not want to sit on Dhomaar's lap? OK. Come then. Take these off and sit on Dhomaar's face then. Let me smell that beautiful pussy of yours again. Let me taste those sweet lips between your legs. Let me—"

"You are *sick*," she muttered as she backed up against him, feeling herself being held in place between his thighs as he unbuttoned her mom jeans and yanked the zipper down, bending his arm up from behind, between her legs, now shoving his hand through the open zipper and rubbing her mound hard and rough.

"Oh, God," she muttered as she felt him pull those jeans down over her bottom even as he massaged her pussy through her panties. "Oh, God, I wanted to talk."

"First you will come for me," he said into her ear from behind as he managed to get those jeans down. He held her standing until she stepped out of those jeans, and then he pulled her back into him, forcing her soft bottom down on his naked, half-erect cock. "Sit on my lap and come for me. Come for Daddy."

"Daddy?" she muttered as she finally sat on his lap and ground her large ass into his cock as he rubbed her pussy so hard through her panties that the soaked cotton rode deep up into her slit. Serious camel-toe. "OK, that's a little disturbing."

"Every little girl wants to come for Daddy," he whispered as he rubbed her clit through her panties, now slowly pushing the waistband down as her feminine smell rose up to the both of them. He inhaled deep as she wriggled her wide hips out of those panties, giggling as he held her tight so she could raise her legs and roll the underwear down past her feet.

"You're so sick," she muttered as she wriggled her naked ass into his cock. "I'm about twenty years and fifty pounds past being anything *close* to a little girl."

"You are Daddy's little girl right now," he growled. "Now spread your legs for Daddy. Let Daddy see if you are clean, if his little girl's pussy is clean for him, wet for him, ready for him. Ready to come for him. At his command."

"Oh, shit," she muttered as she felt his large thumb rest on her clit. Now he placed his forefinger and middle-finger lengthwise along her slit, slowly opening her up as he began to move that thumb in slow, circular motions. "Oh, *God!*"

"Oh, Daddy," he said in a devilish whisper, tapping her clit as he spread the lips of her cunt. "Say Oh, Daddy. Say it."

"Oh," she muttered as her eyelids fluttered and her mouth opened and closed like a fish gasping for air. "Dhomaar this is sick. We're in a *school!*"

"You are in *my* school now," he growled as he slipped the tip of his middle finger just past her wet lower lips, making her pussy clench in that filthy way only he seemed to be able to bring out in her.

And what else was he bringing out in her, Gracie wondered, gasping and sputtering as he slowly pushed that thick middle finger knuckle-deep into her cunt, curling it up against the front wall of her vagina as he massaged her stiff clit in a way that made her eyes roll up in her head as she squirmed and wriggled in his strong arms, in Daddy's strong arms . . .

"You are in *my* school," he said again. "*My* fantasy. My fantasy that you will learn to like, that you will learn to love, that you will learn to need. Now say it. Say *Oh, Daddy*."

"Oh, Daddy," she gurgled as the room faded away. "Oh, Daddy yes."

"Oh, Daddy my pussy is wet for you," he whispered as he slowly slid a second finger into her slit. "Say it."

"Daddy," she muttered. "My pussy . . . my pussy is wet for you. Oh, fuck I'm so wet for you. Wet for you, Daddy."

The fantasy took her with such alarming force that she almost lost track of where she was, of who she was, of who she was with. His presence was so overwhelming, so warm and affectionate, so strangely protective that she leaned her head back and nuzzled her nose up into his warm neck, shamelessly spreading her legs as wide as she could, no trace of self-consciousness, innocently open like a child, a little girl, Daddy's little girl.

"Wet for you, Daddy," she mumbled again, swallowing the last thought of how filthy and twisted this was, how *delightfully* filthy and twisted!

"Let us see," he whispered, sliding those fingers out from her pussy and holding them up so they could both see. She gasped at the clean, glistening wetness that coated his long fingers. Her wetness.

"Oh, Daddy am I wet enough for you?" she whispered as she felt her pussy clench in delightful anticipation. "Am I?"

"Almost," he muttered as she felt his cock harden beneath her ass now. She ground her bum into him harder now, reveling in how quickly he was becoming erect despite his massive climax down her throat not so long ago. "Ah," he groaned now, bucking his cock up into her soft ass as she got him harder. "Ah, you bad little girl. You are getting Daddy hard with what you are doing with your little bottoms. Where did you learn to do that?"

"From Mommy," Grace said without thinking, almost choking with surprise when she heard herself say it. "Mommy taught me. She said Daddy would like it if I did that with my little bottoms. You like it, don't you? You like it, Daddy?"

"Oh, bloody God," he groaned as he grabbed her earlobe between his teeth and growled. His cock was hard like a goddamn rock beneath her grinding ass, and Grace was almost beyond herself with arousal as she felt him lift up her t-shirt and grope her boobs frantically.

His other hand went back down between her legs now, rubbing and grinding, shoving and curling. Now the two of them settled into a frantic rhythm, Gracie grinding on his lap, rubbing Daddy's cock with her little-girl bottom while Daddy fingered her pussy, pinched her pink nipples, told her he was proud of her, that she was making Daddy happy, making Daddy hard, making Daddy horny, horny just like Mommy said to do.

She came then, suddenly, shockingly, with a squeal of surprise as the Sheikh curled those two fingers up inside her and held her tight, pressing down on her clit as she convulsed through an orgasm that arrived silent and sudden but was now rocking her body with a force that threatened to overwhelm her.

"Oh, fuck, I'm coming so hard I can't even . . ." she started to say. But she couldn't finish, because God, that orgasm was somehow still rising, still spiraling upwards, still barreling its way upwards to its peak, a peak that Gracie was suddenly convinced would shatter her, destroy her, perhaps even—

"Daddy's got you," he whispered in her ear as he held her tight against him and let her come. "Keep coming for Daddy like a good little girl. There we go. See how wet your pussy is for Daddy, how tight your cunt is clenching around my fingers, how hard you're coming."

"Oh, *God*!" she wailed as that peak finally hit, *smashing* its way into her goddamn soul it seemed, and her eyes rolled up in her head as she screamed and sobbed, and she was crying in his arms, she thought, dying in his arms, she was sure, reaching heaven under his touch, she was certain, going to hell in this fantasy, she knew.

She came hard, the peak of her climax slowly settling into a pulsating series of secondary orgasms as she whimpered and sobbed in his strong arms. Slowly the madness subsided, and now that protective warmth returned as she realized how secure she felt in his strong arms, how small her body felt against his massive frame, how caring his embrace seemed, how . . . how loving all of it was.

Grace stayed in that protective embrace for what seemed like eternity, smiling and lazily caressing his thick arms as he held her tight. She could feel the breeze against her naked crotch, cool against her cunt as her wetness slowly evaporated. Finally she felt that plastic chair move a bit lower under their weight, and when she looked down she realized with a mortified giggle that the legs were indeed starting to splay out horrifically and it was a wonder she and the Sheikh hadn't gone splat on the floor!

Slowly she pushed herself up to her feet, turning and blinking when she saw how monstrously hard the Sheikh was, his brown cock sticking straight up as he looked up at her and smiled.

"There is no hurry," he said softly, touching her arm, closing and opening his eyes warmly. "We can talk first. Yes?"

Grace blinked as she looked around and tried to get her bearings. She was naked from the waist down. Her t-shirt was stretched badly out of shape from how hard the Sheikh had been groping her boobs. Her bra was pushed up over her tits, which were haphazardly peeking out in raw protest at being manhandled so fiercely by . . . by Daddy.

She almost choked at the memory of what she had been saying, of the filthy fantasy the Sheikh had effortlessly pulled her into. And God, she had come like . . . like she didn't even know what! And she was good at metaphors! Oh, shit, that was insane!

"Um, yeah," she said slowly, standing bare-bottomed in the middle of the staff room now, trying to locate her blue cotton panties. "First I gotta find my panties though."

The Sheikh laughed as he shifted on the chair. He made no effort to help, instead just shrugging and settling in as he shamelessly let his cock—which was now just semi-hard but still thick like a python—hang out in full view.

"Your panties were very wet when I rolled them down your legs," he offered. "I do not think they will be very comfortable to wear."

"I am well aware of the possible panty wetness situation," Grace said firmly as she furrowed her brow and looked in the empty waste basket by the desk. "I still need to *find* them!"

The Sheikh raised both hands and shrugged. Then he exhaled and crossed one leg over the other knee, shrugging again as Grace scratched her head absentmindedly and then started opening the drawers of her desk, as if her panties had somehow crawled in there to dry off.

"Well, OK then," the Sheikh muttered, settling into his chair with a look of amusement, still making no effort to help. "As long as you are well aware."

16

"**I** am well aware of what he must be doing in that school building," Zareena said over the phone to her contact at Habib's security company. "No, there is no need to get *eyes* on them, whatever that means. Just tell me when the Sheikh leaves."

Zareena frowned at her phone and then placed it down on the coffee table in the sunroom of the hotel suite. Then she exhaled hard and stood to full height, placing her hands on her slim hips, grabbing fistfuls of the black satin of her hijab as she clenched and released, walking past Alma and pacing by the window overlooking downtown Tulsa.

"Do not be upset, my queen," Alma said quietly. "It is to our advantage to let him go to her again. It may make things easier when we are faced with the inevitable."

Zareena gave Alma a sharp look, and the petite attendant quickly looked down at her hands, bowing her head for a moment before turning her dark eyes back towards her queen and lover.

"I will decide what is inevitable or not," Zareena said firmly. "What you speak of is a last resort, and you know it. There are other options before we try anything drastic. A lot can happen in nine months."

"This woman will not give up her child for any amount of money, and you know that, my Sheikha," Alma answered, her tone respectful but with an edge.

"We cannot know that," Zareena said with quiet control. "We do not even know her. Perhaps we can break her, get her to accept money, get her to agree to be a surrogate after the fact. The promise of wealth and the guarantee of a wonderful life for her child—with the child's father that too . . . yes, it could sway her if the circumstances are right. If we frame the choice in a convincing way."

"She will not break," said Alma, a grim smile coming to her dark red lips. "We have followed this woman and studied her for six months. We know her as well as anyone. You chose her over the others precisely *because* she was not a woman who would break.

You *wanted* her blood to mix with that of your ancestors. And you *knew* the price to be paid for that. You chose Grace Garner knowing where this would lead. That when the inevitable happened and she laughed at the very mention of giving up rights to her child, then we would need to cross the line between what is just deception and what is illegal. Kidnapping. Coercion. Blackmail. Perhaps more."

"Silence," Zareena rasped, her face twisting with anguish as she turned away from Alma. "We shall not speak of it. Let us pray to Allah and the angels that it does not get to that point. I do not want to seize a child that is not willingly given by the mother."

"But we must be prepared for it," Alma said, standing now and going to Zareena. "Our resolve must be built up."

"You question my resolve, Alma?" the queen said, cocking her head and narrowing her eyes. "Do you know what I have sacrificed for my nation? Do not insult me by questioning my *resolve*! I will do what is needed if the time comes. *If* the time comes."

Alma nodded, looked down at her hands again. "The time is near, which is why I speak of it, my queen. The Sheikh is with her now. For the second time," she said. "And like you said, if he sees her the second time, then there will be a third time, and a fourth, and soon their bond could grow into . . . into . . ."

"Into complications," Zareena said sharply. "Yes.

Surrogate for the Sheikh

My hope was that Dhom could keep it to one night of passion. That way we could have backed off and let her believe she was pregnant by a man who did not give a damn about her and was untouchable in some faraway kingdom. We could have destroyed her financially, made her vulnerable, and then swooped in with the offer to give custody of the child to the father. It could have worked. But now . . ."

"But now the Sheikh has gone to her again," Alma said, sighing. "And so it sets off a different chain of events, does it not, my queen?"

Zareena nodded. "Sadly, yes. And so let Dhomaar take her again, claim her again, fill her, flay her, fist her, fuck her. Let him even love her, if that is what emerges. It will make things complicated. But the result will be the same, just with more pain for everyone. I will manage the situation. And you are correct, Alma. Perhaps it does make things easier. At least this way we will not need to have Habib's people following this woman for the next nine months."

Alma nodded as she met the queen's gaze. "So we are moving forward?"

"Yes," said Zareena. "The arrangements have been made in the Royal Palace?"

"Southern wing," said Alma, nodding again. "Just as you asked."

Zareena nodded once. The North wing was where she and Dhom held court. It contained the sprawling banquet halls and the towering domes under which the ministers gathered. It was the only part of the palace open to the public, and there were museum rooms and visitors' gardens, marble fountains that lit up at night, and sprawling prayer rooms for the holiest of events when the Sheikh and Sheikha led their people in ritual.

The East wing held Zareena's private day-rooms. The West wing belonged to the Sheikh and his daytime activities. But the Southern wing was only used after sunset. It held the Sheikh and Sheikha's most private chambers, accessible only to the most trusted attendants. The Southern wing, which would now hold a new guest—for at least the next nine months.

"You do realize," Alma said, smiling as she tried to break the heavy mood in the room. "That kidnapping a white woman and making her bear a child in captivity is . . . like they say . . . a bit stereotypical for us savages of the desert."

Zareena snorted as her eyes lit up and she allowed herself a moment of lightness. "Ya Allah, yes. Embarrassingly so. But at least this time it is the elegant queen doing it, not the savage king!"

"That is a nice twist to the old story, my queen," said Alma, bowing her head and gliding towards her room to prepare for their journey home. "Well done."

Yes, well done, Dhomaar, Zareena thought as she sighed and folded her arms across her chest. Your royal cock and caveman balls may give both of you pleasure right now, but are only going to cause pain and sadness when all is said and done. So enjoy the next nine months, my Sheikh. Enjoy the woman who will bear your child. You deserve some romance in your lonely life, I suppose.

17

"Well, that's romantic," said Grace. "So your wife is your second cousin and she's also a lesbian. So she's totally cool with you doing whatever the hell you want. Wonderful. Good for you."

The Sheikh looked down at his cock as he shifted on the plastic chair that was far too small for his frame and in fact felt like it might simply collapse under the weight of his muscle. He hadn't bothered to put his pants back on, and now that he looked closer, neither had she. Hah! He smiled with a rising affection as he watched Grace lean back in her red swivel chair, sitting behind her very official-looking desk and speaking authoritatively to him. She hadn't been able to find her panties, and had given up and sat down behind her desk, placing those crumpled jeans over her crotch and thighs as they talked.

Dhomaar had told her only what he dared—even though now he realized he had just revealed a secret held by only three people: Zareena, Alma, and himself! Still, it was far better than telling her the full truth. Which was what, by the way? Even *he* was not sure right now—now that he had vetoed the plan of staying the hell away from this woman and letting Zareena's scheme play out as designed. So what was *his* plan now? Clearly they were past the point of a one-night stand—and not just technically speaking but emotionally speaking as well, it felt like! Ya Allah, Zareena was right! Just by giving in to my need a second time, perhaps I am done for!

Gracie was rocking in her chair now, her voice rising in confidence as she looked up and to the left like the wheels were turning behind those big brown eyes. "But you're not allowed to divorce," she said like a teacher recapping the day's lesson. "And you're not allowed to have any more wives either. So what does that make me?"

Dhomaar raised an eyebrow. "Ah, so you would be ready to be my second wife, my proud American schoolteacher, role model to feminists of the future?"

"What? No! Of *course* not," she said quickly, frowning and turning red before looking away and averting her eyes down. "I wouldn't even be your *first* wife, buddy," she added jokingly, hastily forcing a smile.

Dhomaar nodded once and smiled, not pushing any harder when he saw how red her pretty round cheeks were. Ah, this woman, he thought. She is such a woman. So wonderfully female. So gorgeously feminine. Already her mind wonders what comes next! Where is this going? Where do things lead? What does the sex mean? Can I see myself married to him? Do I see myself having his baby? Carrying his child?

But now the smile faded from the Sheikh's dark face as he narrowed his eyes and looked past Gracie. How could he tell her? How could he *ever* tell her? It was already too late, was it not? Because now he actually *cared* what she thought of him! He shouldn't care, but somehow he did care. Ya Allah, Zareena was right! My wise queen knew this would happen, did she not? And I followed my throbbing cock and swinging balls anyway! Now there is no way out without hurting this woman when she finds she has been used. No way out without myself feeling the hurt when I see how her expression changes as the truth comes out, see those big brown eyes go wide with sadness and then narrow with anger. Perhaps even hatred!

But think, Dhomaar. Now that you have a sense of this woman, think about what she will do when the truth does come out. What will Grace Garner say to

Queen Zareena when the offer is made for the child? Will she say, "Yes, of course you can take my baby in exchange for cash?" Will she shrug and say, "No, it's fine that you didn't tell me I was going to be a surrogate until after I got pregnant. No problem, Queen Zareena and Sheikh Dhomaar! I understand your traditions and beliefs, and I too believe that this was a much better idea than to simply hire a surrogate mother to carry Dhomaar's child. Where are the custody papers? Here, I will sign immediately!"

Dhomaar chewed on his knuckle so hard it almost drew blood when he realized that God, this woman was not going to break even under the considerable force of Zareena's will! Zareena might believe in her own power, but this time the Sheikha was wrong. She might have "researched" Grace Garner, but she did not "know" Grace Garner. Not like he knew her, the Sheikh thought.

So what now? What do you do now, Dhomaar? Think, goddamn it!

"I won't even be your first wife," came her words again, repeated in the swirl of Dhomaar's mind as he glanced at Grace and then up at the ceiling.

Slowly a tingle of clarity and hope emerged in the Sheikh as he narrowed those green eyes and looked at Gracie again. She was too strong-willed to break under the psychological games Zareena might throw at her. But the Sheikh did not play such tiresomely convoluted games, did he? No. The Sheikh simply decided what he wanted and then made sure the world and everything in it conformed to his will. Then he took what he wanted. It is mine and I take it. I am Sheikh. I am king. I am ruler.

So perhaps I can convince this woman to do the unthinkable. Perhaps I can get her to . . . to . . . ya Allah, do I dare? Do I dare say the words that are bubbling up in me even as I try to choke them back as the words of a madman?

He clenched his fist again and bit down on that knuckle, and then he lowered his hand and took a breath and spoke.

"I can promise you everything but marriage," he said to her in a steady, low voice, the depth of emotion that came with it shaking him. "Gracie, I can promise you everything a man has to offer his woman. Everything. But I cannot give you marriage."

"Sorry, what?" she said, frowning because he had interrupted her mid-sentence—though the Sheikh had no memory of what she had been saying. Perhaps wondering about the panty situation again.

"Everything but the wedding," he said. "Decide now or forever hold your tongue."

And the Sheikh grinned like a lunatic as he felt a strange madness take over, like now that damned universe was speaking to *him*—perhaps speaking *through* him! He rose from his seat now, the strained legs of his plastic throne springing back to shape as the king stood in the streaming sunlight of the Wilson Park Middle School staff room, cock and balls swinging beneath his open shirt-tails as he walked towards Gracie, who appeared close to having a brain-stroke that had frozen her face in a pretzel-like twist of absolute shock.

"Um, decide what," she stammered, turning her head to the left even as she kept her eyes on him. "Decide whether you're dangerously insane or just regular insane? I'll have to think about that for a moment."

"Do not mock me," he said loudly, placing his bare foot on that plastic chair and pointing at the ceiling. "I am a goddamn king!"

"Yeah, well, I already told you: This is the realm of Gracie the Ruler," she said, glancing furtively at his cock and balls, which were on prominent display as the Sheikh stood there, his foot on that poor plastic chair. "And I command you to stop talking absolute *nonsense!*" She snorted and shook her head, exhaling hard as if she had just convinced herself that he was indeed joking.

"It is not a joke, Grace," he said now, putting his leg down and reaching for his pants without taking his eyes off her. "Look at me, Gracie. *Look* at me!"

She looked up into his eyes now, blinking and looking away again before taking a breath and holding his gaze. Now the Sheikh could see it in her eyes. He could see something that made his heart leap, made his soul soar, made his body feel light like a goddamn feather! Ya Allah, he could see in her what he felt in himself: That there was something here. That there was *everything* here!

"I don't know how to even . . ." she started to say before she just shook her head and looked away from his eyes. "OK, listen. I don't know if you're serious or—"

"By *God* I am serious!" he shouted, narrowing his eyes as his jaw went tight. "Stop denying what we both feel! You are pregnant, and you know it. You carry my seed in your womb, and you can damned well feel it! So just—"

"Wait, what?" she said, almost doubling over in shock. "Where the hell did *that* come from? Pregnant? Are you . . . I mean . . . Oh, shit, we are not even . . ."

She stood now, shaking her head furiously as she straightened her crumpled jeans and tried to step into them. She put one leg through and then stood up and stared at him. "OK, seriously, you are just *way* past the point of—"

But then she stopped abruptly, freezing and cocking her head to the side as her eyes turned to the left.

"*Past* the point? I am not even *close* to the point, and I—" he started to shout.

"Quiet!" she whispered, raising her hand as those jeans fell to the floor. "Oh, shit, that's the elevator doors! Someone's coming. OK, we need to hide. *Now*! Follow me!"

She desperately tried to get those jeans back on, but the legs were all twisted up and she stumbled and would have fallen if the Sheikh hadn't stepped forward and grabbed her.

"Screw it," she whispered, kicking the jeans away as they heard the sound of keys right outside the staff room door. "Come on, Dhomaar. That door over there. Run!"

The Sheikh stared in amused disbelief as Grace Garner ran towards a metal door marked "Exit," the globes of her magnificently naked bottoms bouncing with urgency. Then he looked at his own trousers and underwear crumpled on the floor, and with a shrug he took off after his woman, cock and balls swinging with glee as those creatures of fantasy finally arrived on the scene, earnestly whispering to each other that this gon' be good.

18

"What good will this do?" the Sheikh said, snorting as he held up the flimsy purple scarf that Gracie had handed him with instructions to use to hide his shame so they could make their way downstairs and run for the Sheikh's limousine. "I am to wear it like a loincloth? Like I am some Indian guru?"

"Well, it's all I have," Gracie said, rummaging through the miscellany on the tall shelving that ran along the side wall of her home-room class. "Unless you want those woolen socks that have been here since last winter."

Gracie had led the Sheikh down the emergency exit—whose alarm had thankfully stopped working a decade ago—and the two had snuck into her classroom on the second floor, where she thought she had at least some semblance of clothing that would perhaps let them leave without being arrested and registered as sex offenders if they were seen before they made it to the safety of that limousine and its tinted glass.

"I coulda sworn I had left a pair of sweat pants here," she muttered as she pulled out a sheath of old drawing paper with some very bad stick figures done in black Sharpie. "Shit, no. I wore those home last month after I spilled grape-soda all over my . . . OK, you know what? You're gonna have to use the scarf," she said in a fit of anxiety, tossing those drawings back on the shelf and turning to the Sheikh, hands on her hips, legs together, eyes up front and center. "And this is my goddamn *career* we're talking about. So you will damn well do what I say, got it?"

The Sheikh frowned and held up the purple scarf again, looking hard into her eyes before holding a straight face and nonchalantly tossing the scarf over his shoulder. "I am not covering my royal cock with your silly purple scarf."

Gracie exhaled hard, trying to calm herself down. She had crouched outside the exit door and listened to see who it was, and when she heard a woman's voice muttering something about how it smelled weird in the staff room, Gracie's worst fears were confirmed: It was Ms. Walters herself.

Now Gracie wondered if she was going to faint, and she looked around the empty classroom while breathing deep, gulping down lungfuls of oxygen, telling herself that people faint because they stop breathing deep when they're stressed and so if she just took deep breaths she'd be fine. Sure enough, several breaths later she knew she sure as hell wasn't going to faint, and in fact she wasn't even as doomed as she had thought. This was her home classroom and the door was locked now. Ms. Walters wasn't even going to come down to this floor, let alone knock on the door. As long as they stayed put—and quiet—they could just wait it out. Yup. Simple. Just sit tight and wait.

Now she turned to the Sheikh, who seemed least concerned that he was a six-foot-five Arab, naked from the waist down, strolling around an American public school in the middle of the day. Did anything phase this man? God, he was so annoyingly calm! Was he actually reading those pinned-up compositions written by her ten-year-olds?!

He laughed now, glancing towards her and pointing at the bulletin board with the scrawled-out essays. "Ah, children are truly delightful, yes?" he said with a big, goofy grin as Gracie stared at him in wonder, her frustration slowly turning to amusement, her anxiety gradually giving way to a calmness that allowed her to step back for a moment and laugh at how ridiculous this was.

"Which one is that?" she said, smiling as she walked over to him and squinted up at the composition on the board. "Oh, God, that's Emma. She's a precocious little kid. Smart as hell." Now Gracie's face lit up as she was reminded of the earnest innocence of these ten-year olds who saw the world with such clarity, it seemed sometimes. "Oh, but read this one. It's by little Michael. Adorable, yeah?"

The Sheikh read it and laughed, putting his arm around Gracie and pulling her close, the two of them joined at the hip as they read the words of ten-year-olds and giggled and clapped like they were kids themselves. Slowly they moved along the decorated walls of Gracie's classroom, the Sheikh asking about cards and compositions, the artwork and the collages. Gracie smiled with him and laughed with him, snuggled into him when he pulled her close, giggled when he patted her naked bottom.

Soon they were kissing, just like that, just kissing in the middle of class, lips locked, tongues wagging, lovers tasting each other, testing each other, taking each other . . . taking each other to that place where the arousal reigned supreme, where their desire for each other moved to the forefront, where his shaft hardened and her pussy tightened, where his cock rose up against her mound and her vagina oozed its welcoming wetness.

Now he was inside her, his cock sliding in with shocking ease as he backed her up against the shelving and kissed her deep as he started to pump.

"Oh, God, Dhomaar," she gasped when she saw that without even realizing it she was hot, wet, spread, and being taken again. "Oh, shit, that feels good."

"Yes, it feels good, Gracie," he growled as he thrust slow and firm, looking her right in the eye as he drew back from the kiss and placed his hand behind her head so she wouldn't hurt herself against the wall. "Bloody hell, it feels good. Good like last night, yes?"

"Yes," she sighed as she felt him flex his cock deep inside her. "Shit, yes!"

"And it will feel good when we do it again tomorrow?" he whispered as he pumped into her one more time.

"Yes," she sighed again as she felt him raise her left leg by the thigh and start to thrust harder. "Oh, my *God*, Dhomaar! Don't stop."

"I will not stop," he grunted now, pushing harder as she felt him somehow grow inside her, his girth expanding the walls of her cunt, it felt like. "I will never stop. Tomorrow. Next week. Next month. I will keep coming. Keep going. Deeper, harder, longer. Like this, like this, and like *this*!"

Surrogate for the Sheikh

Now he *rammed* up into her and she *howled* with the force of his thrust, digging her nails into the back of his neck as she opened her mouth wide to receive his hungry kiss. He kissed her hard as he started to pump with force, drive with gusto, ram with purpose.

"Again and again," he panted into her hair as she moaned and whimpered. "Every day, every week, every month. Never stop. Cannot stop. I will take you every day. Make you mine every day. Every *goddamn* day, Gracie. Even when your belly is large and round with our child I will take you."

"What?" she muttered through her tears of ecstasy as he pumped into her. "What child?"

"You are pregnant," he growled into her as he thrust again. "You know it, and I know it."

She giggled through her next groan. "You're mad, you know that? God, you're just—"

Now suddenly he pulled back and grabbed her by the hair from behind, pulling her head back and making her look up at him. "You think I am mad? You think I am joking? Do you not feel my seed inside you already? Do you not sense that last night we conceived a child?"

Grace stared up at him as she felt a sickening chill go through her with his words. Her arousal was so strong she wasn't sure if she was hearing him correctly, wasn't sure if she was understanding him right, wasn't sure if this weird tingle was just the arousal or something else.

She looked into his eyes, frowning as his words from last night rang through her head. "I have waited six months." "The best of me is in you now." "Six months for this." "Now it is done."

It is done? What is done? Am I going mad, she thought as she swore she saw the answer in his green eyes, felt the answer behind her own eyes, inside her own body, in the way she had reacted to him, the way she was reacting now.

"This is insane," she gasped, feeling like the walls were closing in on her. "No one can know that. You can't know that. I can't know that. It's insane, Dhomaar. OK, listen, maybe we need to take a step back and—"

"Back?" he said, snorting as he looked down at her. "*Back*?! Ya Allah, you disappoint me, Grace. You are ignoring what you know is true."

"Ignoring *what*?" she screamed now, not caring who the hell heard. "Some magical knowledge that I'm pregnant from last night? Dhomaar, it's scientifically *impossible* to know that right now! It's goddamn *impossible*! You're speaking as if you know for sure already. There's no way we can be certain this soon!"

Now the Sheikh let go of her hair and pulled his cock out of her, and Gracie felt a hollow sensation of anguish whip through her, like her own body was screaming in rage, raging at her ignorance, spitting in her face with disgust at how she was willfully ignoring the wisdom of her vessel, the flesh-and-blood vessel which was the seat of her soul in this lifetime.

"All right, Grace," the Sheikh growled now, pacing the empty classroom as he took off his white shirt and tossed it aside. He stood naked now, brown and hard, ridges of muscle rippling in the light shadows of the classroom. "All right. Now you have done it. Now you have unleashed what I have held back. You have awakened me, and now you will pay the price."

This was the first time Gracie had actually seen the Sheikh without his shirt, and the sight floored her as her jaw drooped with astonishment. The man truly was sculpted by the gods, with striations of beautiful brown muscle lining his abdomen, pectorals like slabs of heavy granite, shoulders like ridges of rock, arm muscles defined so well she could teach a goddamn anatomy class with him as the main exhibit.

His cock was hard, swollen, supremely erect, and it bounced stiffly as he walked towards her. Slowly she backed up, wondering what the hell was about to happen.

"No, listen," she muttered weakly as her pussy clenched and released, a fresh flow of wetness oozing from her slit. "I'm not thinking straight. Let's just talk about . . . about . . ." She frowned as she tried to remember what they had been talking about, but she suddenly couldn't. She closed her eyes tight to regain focus, and now it came back to her: that madness about her already being pregnant; those weird statements when he fucked her last night; all this stuff about carrying his seed, carrying the best of him, the best of his line, about how he *knew* they had conceived last night. Madness! And now *she* was going to pay the price? *What* price?

Now suddenly she felt him *grab* her by the hair, and before she could get her balance the Sheikh *dragged* her across the room and pushed her down to her knees facing the old-style metal radiator pipes by the far wall. She gasped and tried to turn, but he stood above her, holding her in place between his muscular thighs, now pushing her down until her legs were bent beneath her, her face close to the pipes lining the wall.

"Dhomaar, what the hell—" she started to say.

But she swallowed the words as she felt him grab her wrists and pull her arms out in front of her, that purple scarf coming down and twisting around those wrists, pulled tight with astonishing speed, wound hard around the radiator pipe, double-knotted and pulled tight again until holy mother of God she was tied to the goddamn radiator, on her fucking knees, the Sheikh above her, behind her, in control of her.

"OK, very funny," she said weakly as a combination of panic and the most shocking arousal whipped through her. "Haha. Now just—"

And she gagged and flicked her eyes open wide as the Sheikh pulled her head back by her hair and stuffed that woolen sock of hers into her mouth as she tried to scream. He leaned in and checked as if to make sure it wouldn't choke her, and then he stepped back.

She pulled against her soft purple cuffs as she tried to turn her head and see him, but the bindings were tight, almost professional, and only now did it truly sink in that she couldn't break free at all. She tried to turn to him but couldn't do that either. She breathed in and out desperately until she managed to convince herself she wasn't going to choke to death. Then she sat there helpless and bound for what seemed like a long time, until finally she felt his presence behind her.

The Sheikh slowly walked around and stood by the radiator, arms folded across his heavy, muscled chest. "In my classroom I do not tolerate so much back-talk," he said in a low, deep voice that sent a shiver right down the middle of Gracie's body, from her neck through her back, down past her quivering buttocks and her shaking thighs. "It is tiresome and quite unnecessary. If you have some doubts that you are pregnant, then I will clear up those doubts, my little science teacher. I will take you again and again, fill you again and again, when I want, as often as I want, as deep and hard and rough as I want. Then you can calculate the probabilities and analyze the chances. Eventually your calculations will tell you what I am already telling you, what your body is already telling you."

She coughed as she tried to speak, blinking as she looked up at this madman who seemed to be saying he was going to keep her tied up and gagged until he had successfully impregnated her.

But he kept talking. "Of course, it will not be as simple as that, Gracie. Because of your back-talk and defiance, the mocking tone in which you questioned my conclusions, the disrespect you have shown not only to a King and Sheikh but to the father of your unborn child... yes, because of that you will need to be taught a thing or two about how my world works. You will need to learn the discipline that Sheikh Dhomaar demands. I will teach you the discipline that Sheikh Dhomaar demands. So, Ms. Grace Garner, although on the surface it appears we are in your classroom, the truth is that you are in my school. The School of Sheikh Dhomaar. The lesson will begin shortly. It may smart a little, but you will be better for it, I assure you. Now you think about that until I return."

Now he turned his head and looked to the left, smirking and briskly walking out of her sight. She heard the sound of plaster tearing, like something was being ripped off the wall, and when the Sheikh came back into view, Gracie almost fainted at the sight.

Because here was the Sheikh, naked and hard, rippling muscle and throbbing veins, black Arabic letters tattooed down the side of his torso . . . yes, here he was with that long, thick, heavy wooden ruler in his hand, the one that had been nailed up on the wall, the one that was three feet long and several inches wide, with the words "Gracie the Ruler" carefully painted in black acrylic.

"You're fucking kidding me," she tried to say, but of course it sounded like, "Broiuokdhfsdfwee" and so she shut up and tried to signal with her eyes that enough was enough and there was no way in bloody hell he was going to—

SMACK, came the first strike, arriving swift and silent on her upturned ass, and her eyes almost popped out of their sockets at the stinging pain that spread through her buttocks so fast she almost fainted.

"Woothefooocck!" she mumbled through that woolen sock.

SMACK! was the response on her stinging buttocks.

"Ddddontttyouuffuccckkinggdaarree!" she gargled.

SMACK, SMACK! was the reply.

"Illlkilllyouooo!" she choked.

SMACK, SMACK, SMACK!! was the retort.

And then she understood the lesson, and Gracie the Ruler shut the hell up and she arched her back down and stuck those bottoms up in the air, closing her eyes tight as the Sheikh brought that wooden paddle down *hard*, again and again, smacking clean and straight, right on the beautiful meat of her upturned bum.

And she kept that ass turned up and out, and she bowed her head, and she enjoyed it.

Oh mother of God, she enjoyed it.

19

He left that sock in her mouth even after he gave her the last smack she deserved. Then he tossed the quivering ruler aside, leaning in and kissing her upturned bottoms that were red and raw, the ruler marks clearly visible as long, straight red lines on those magnificent globes.

He massaged her buttocks as she whimpered and sobbed, kissing the back of her thighs as he reached between her legs and rubbed her pussy, smiling when he felt how wet she was, how warm she was, how *his* she was.

"All done," he whispered as he slowly massaged

his cock with one hand while rubbing her pussy and licking her along her rear crack. "How's my baby girl? You were so good as you took your punishment. Daddy's proud of you. Daddy's proud of you for keeping your bottoms so straight and tight as you got what you deserved."

She whimpered again as he pushed two fingers into her cunt from beneath, spreading those lips and leaning in from behind and gently blowing warm air against her pubic curls. Grace moaned through that sock, pulled on her binds, arched her back lower and spread those thick thighs as she turned her pussy back and out towards him.

Ya Allah, she is so ready, he thought as he massaged his balls and glanced at her red velvet slit, open and wet, long and magnificent, delicate brown hairs lining the outside, highlighting the entry-point for his throbbing cock. Oh, God, I will never tire of taking her. I know it. To say I feel bonded to this woman is to mock the depth of my physical need for her.

He leaned in and took a deep breath of her feminine aroma, shuddering as he filled his lungs with her scent. Now he licked her as those smooth round buttocks quivered against his face. He licked her again, now running his tongue up along her rear crack, slowly parting her buttcheeks as she moaned and tensed up. With a groan he spread her cheeks wide, glancing at her dark rear shadow, his breath catching when he took in the sight of her tight rear hole. He licked her pucker now, circling her asshole with his tongue as she clenched her buttocks and tightened up, trying to close him out. But he held her asscheeks wide apart, licking her circle again, now pushing the tip of his tongue in as she clenched again and tried to turn her head as she whimpered desperately into her gag.

He pushed her head back facing forward, licking her again, coating her asshole with saliva and then sliding his middle finger into her ass as he felt her clamp her buttocks together as she once again screamed something through her gag.

"Relax, baby girl," he muttered as he held that finger steady inside her bum. "Daddy knows what he's doing. I will not hurt my baby. I love my baby."

She whimpered as he said it, and now the Sheikh felt her buttocks relax as she opened up for him. Soon he was sliding his finger in and out of her rear pucker, and she was beginning to move with him, moan with his grunts, whimper with his whispers. He smacked her buttocks lightly as he pumped his finger into her, smacked harder now, rubbed and kneaded, coaxed as she pleaded.

Soon his cock was so hard he was certain he would explode all over her back and buttocks if he did not give her pussy what it was so clearly demanding from between her legs. But still he held on, closing his eyes as he felt her arousal build along with his. This was more than just him taking what he wanted, he reminded himself. It was more than him just giving her what she wanted, he told himself. This was truly a lesson. There was indeed learning taking place. She was learning about herself even as she learned about him. She was getting a glimpse of how twisted he could be, and at the same time learning the shocking truth of how much she could enjoy being twisted along with him.

Of course, that sort of teaching and learning happened with all the girls, all the women. But there was something more here, was there not? Something more at stake, it felt like. After all, he had asked her a question that was . . . ya Allah, it was almost a marriage proposal, was it not?!

"I can promise you everything a man can give," he had said with all the seriousness he had. "But I cannot give you marriage. Everything but marriage."

In a twisted way, he *was* giving her marriage, was he not? Promising to be with her and her alone. Father her children. Protect her. Care for her. Raise a family with her. Grow old with her. By God, that is what he had meant, was it not? And was that not marriage? Everything but the wedding!

Would she accept that? he wondered as he looked down at this magnificent woman tied and bound before him, spread wide and streaked red.

"Everything but the wedding," he said out loud

now. "I can promise you anything and everything, but I cannot give you that."

Now she turned her head halfway and he could see her eyes. They were tear-filled and narrowed to slits, but there was a focus coming to them as he spoke. So he kissed the small of her back now, massaging her buttocks again, spreading her as he went down on his knees behind her. He guided his cock to her slit, sliding in and flexing, holding his length in there as he watched her eyes roll up in her head. Soon she turned and faced the wall again, head lowered as the arousal took her.

He started to thrust now, asking her the question again, whispering the words, pumping harder as he slowly reached for that purple scarf and undid her knots, now unplugging her gag as she gasped. He pulled out his cock and quickly turned her body, sitting himself cross-legged on the classroom floor and guiding her onto his upright cock, smiling as she squatted down over his erection, slowly lowering her heavy body onto his throne.

He groaned as he watched his thick, glistening shaft disappear into her, and he felt so deep inside her that he almost exploded right then and there. She rode him now as he grabbed her hips and buttocks, lifting her and pulling her back down, harder now, faster now, deeper now, until she was raising herself up and then *crashing* down on his cock, *screaming* as all her weight added to the force of his hard cock re-entering her.

Together they rode, up and down, in and out, the desks and chairs near them rattling as they moved across the floor, the Sheikh *ripping* off her t-shirt and tossing her bra away, *devouring* her hanging tits as she clawed at his hair, bounced on his cock.

Finally he felt her come, her bouncing body seizing up as she let out a long wail of ecstasy, tears flowing down her round cheeks as he pumped and clenched and sucked on her nipples. Soon he was there too, while she was still wailing and clenching, legs wrapped around his hard waist, arms hugging him so damned tight, her eyes closed all the way.

He came silently as he held her, gritting his teeth as he felt his semen blast up like a volcano inside her, filling her skies with his heat, flooding her plains with his seed.

"Oh, God, Gracie," he muttered as he pumped and flexed even as she barely moved from her viselike embrace. "Gracie, are you all right?"

She was quiet as he shuddered through his climax, groaning and grunting as he throbbed and flexed, balls seizing, cock pumping, finally slowing down into short little gasps as he exhaled hard and listened for her heartbeat, wondering if she had died on him, she was so goddamn still!

"I think you're right," she finally whispered against

his neck as his cock squeezed out the last of his load and she emerged from that post-coital embrace.

"About what?" he muttered.

"About last night," she said, slowly pulling her head back so she could look at him. "About being pregnant. About how my body already knows even if my mind thinks it's impossible to know yet."

"Ah, you have chosen to agree with me," he said, raising an eyebrow and glancing at that wooden ruler that sat patiently to their left. "What brought you to that conclusion?"

"Well," she said, raising an eyebrow herself and cocking her head as she looked him in the eye. "It's the only possible explanation for why I feel this overwhelming urge to be with a man who is sexist, violent, twisted, and generally quite scary and perhaps even dangerous."

"That bad?" he said, grinning as he touched his nose to hers.

"Yes, you *are* that bad," she whispered through a smile.

"I wasn't asking if I was that bad," he said. "I was just confirming that your *need* for me is that bad."

"I hate you," she said as he kissed her cheek.

"Hate is the first sign of love," he said, kissing her again.

"I don't think we're there yet."

"Where? Hate? Or love?"

"Oh, God, Dhomaar. This is ... this feels ... I mean, there's no rush to decide anything, yes? I mean, we still barely know each—"

"We have our entire unmarried lives to get to know each other, whatever the bloody hell that means," the Sheikh snapped. "Ya Allah, we have shared the most intimate parts of ourselves, and your sticking point is that we do not know each other's favorite colors or list of allergies or pet peeves or whatever else you consider part of getting to know each other. Should we do some Facebook personality quizzes to speed up the process?"

"You know those quizzes are just a way for companies to develop psychological profiles of people so they can sell that information to advertisers."

The Sheikh sighed as he pretended to push her away, and she giggled and snuggled closer. He turned his face towards the window as he listened to her ramble on, and his thoughts drifted to a nagging fear that favorite colors and pet peeves aside, there would be a part of him she could never get to know—at least not if he wanted to actually be with this woman. After all, if she ever found out she had been tracked and followed, profiled and picked, selected and seduced ...

And now he thought of Zareena, and his breathing quickened as he wondered what the hell she was planning. After all, she would know he had gone into the school building. She would know he had gone back

Surrogate for the Sheikh

to Grace even after she warned him not to. And Zareena was not one to leave things to chance, so certainly she had accounted for this situation. So what would Zareena do, now that she knew Dhom had "given in to his need" and gone to Grace, taken her again, would keep taking her!

Ya Allah, Zareena will take her, came the thought from the darkest part of his mind, the part of his mind where paranoia sat quietly in the shadows, alert but silent, waiting to be summoned so it could leap into the light, bringing all the madness that came with it.

Bloody hell, of course Zareena will take her! Now that I have effectively destroyed Zareena's negotiating position, the Sheikha will find a way to strengthen that position again. And what better way than to take this woman out of her comfort zone, out of her life, out of her goddamn mind perhaps!

For a moment the Sheikh almost panicked, but although a healthy paranoia did exist in this king, panic was not his domain. So he stayed with this woman and let the thoughts flow through him like the afternoon breeze . . . thoughts and options, tactics and strategies, means and ends. Of course he trusted Zareena as far as her motives went: She was in service of their kingdom, their land, their people, and she would follow that motivation through all its twists and turns, loops and winds.

But what are *my* motives, the Sheikh wondered as

that afternoon breeze flowed through Grace's open brown hair as she laughed with him, smiled with him, danced with him in the gentle aftermath of their coupling. *Am I truly focused only on what's best for Mizra and the future of my kingdom? Or am I reaching for something that I want for myself? Am I convincing myself that it is OK to be selfish and take this woman for my own instead of staying with the plan and letting her pass as a one-night stand?*

Everything but marriage, came the thought again on the whispering wind, and the Sheikh frowned as a strange clarity came to him. *By God*, he thought, *stop thinking like a fool in love and start thinking like a king who always gets what he wants. You will have it all, Dhomaar. The woman, the heir, and the future security of the nation. She* will *agree to be your woman without the stamp of marriage. It may take time, but she* will *break, she* will *submit, she* will *say yes to this marriage proposal that involves everything but marriage.*

And by God, if Zareena is mad enough, determined enough, dedicated enough to have a plan to seize this woman, then it is not just Zareena who will gain the advantage in negotiations. I will have an advantage too, will I not?

And I will need the advantage to make this proud American woman submit to my will. She is smart and modern and not some hopelessly idealistic romantic, but she is a woman. By *God*, she is a woman! And every woman wishes for a wedding, muses on her marriage, dreams of that first dance with her handsome groom. It will be hard to take that dream away from her. But what can I do?

You can step down from the throne, divorce Zareena, and take Grace to be your wife, came the thought. Of course, by law Zareena will also be stripped of the Sheikhood, and the Royal Council will be left scrambling to convince one of the fat and happy billionaires of our scattered family to come back and be a reluctant ruler. Even if that mad old Sheikh Kalyan makes no attempt to invade, the kingdom of Mizra would almost certainly fade away into history with no strong leader to hold the spirit of the land together. Newer generations would take their wealth and leave for the larger cities in mainland Arabia and the West. The population would dwindle. The optimism of the people would depart, leaving a barren race of old Mizrahi faithfuls. In fifty years Mizra would return to the desert. Turn to salt.

Yes, I could do that, the Sheikh thought with a scornful grimace, laughing at himself for even allowing such an option to *exist* in his proud mind. He had made his commitment to the kingdom of Mizra and to its people the day he chose to marry Zareena and take his place as Sheikh and King. That commitment would never waver. Not for a promise of eternal life.

Not under threat of painful death. Not for a woman. Not even for this woman.

And you know what, the Sheikh thought as he glanced at Grace in her naked beauty, brown hair like a gold halo in the sunbeams of the Oklahoma afternoon, this woman would never *let* me make that choice for her. I know it even though I do not know her favorite goddamn color!

So that is it, he thought in the sudden way all great leaders make the most monumental of decisions. I have decided. I am Sheikh and I will have it all. All but the marriage. She is coming with me, and that is all.

"Purple," he blurted out.

"What?" she said.

"Your favorite color. It is purple."

"Um, no. It's actually green."

The Sheikh shrugged and nodded. "You are right. We will need a little time to get to know each other. Nine months, shall we say? You can pack tonight, and we leave in the morning. But pack light. In three months you will not fit into these clothes. We will have maternity clothes woven by the royal tailors, and—"

"Whoa, whoa, *whoa!*" she said, like she was aghast and amused, perhaps even a bit afraid at how matter-of-factly the Sheikh issued his statements, like this was not a question, perhaps not even a conversation. "I have a job. A career. There's still a couple of weeks of school left before we break for summer, but even after that I've got—"

"Your only job for the next nine months is to carry my child," he grunted as her eyes went wide in shock.

"OK, this is why we cannot have a real conversation," she sputtered, blinking with indignation. "I spend every day teaching young girls that their careers come first, their ambitions come first, their dreams and—"

"It is not your dream to have a child?" the Sheikh asked now, narrowing his green eyes as he held her gaze.

Gracie blinked hard and swallowed. "Well, no . . . I mean, that's not what I meant. I mean, important dreams like careers, and ambitions, and—"

"So the dream to have a child is in your view a lower class of dream? If a girl says her most cherished dream is to bear children and be a wonderful mother, you will shut her down and say that the dream is unworthy of pursuing? That all other dreams must come before that?" The Sheikh sat up straight now, feeling a serene determination driving his voice. In truth he had never consciously deliberated on such things in much depth, but now that his mind was turning to the matters of babies and motherhood, parenting and fatherhood, the words seemed to flow with shocking ease.

Gracie blinked and looked down at her hands for a

moment, and the Sheikh could see her jaw set tight. "I don't want to talk about it," she said quietly, looking up at him with a vaguely puzzled expression, like she was questioning something, perhaps answering something.

But he waited in silence, and finally she nodded, reaching out and playfully punching his rock-hard chest. "It's complicated being a woman in today's America," she said softly, eyes darting left and right, like she was hoping no one would hear. "It's important to remember that a woman is more than a goddamn womb with two boobs, and I try to teach that to my girls. I mean, sure, yeah, even though a lot of women have no interest in having kids, most women do at some point feel that need. And no, it's certainly not a *low class* dream! I mean, if anything it's a high . . . the highest . . . it's . . . God, you're so . . . so . . . what are you smiling at?!"

"Womb and two boobs." the Sheikh said, raising an eyebrow.

Gracie turned red. "Well, yeah. What about it?"

The Sheikh shrugged. "Well, I have always been a buttocks man myself," he said, drawing back and covering his face as she *swiped* at him. "OK, stop. Stop. You will break my nose! Stop, or I will pick up that ruler again. I am warning you for the last time, woman! Don't make me pick up that ruler!"

She stopped now, and when the Sheikh lowered

his hands he saw her sitting with her knees tucked under her, boobs hanging free, face going red with embarrassment as she glanced at that ruler and then back at the Sheikh.

"You'll pick up that ruler again?" she said in a low whisper, slowly rising to her knees, spreading her legs, bending forward onto her elbows now. She arched her back down as the Sheikh felt his cock go to full-mast with painful urgency. Then she blinked and took a breath like she was steeling herself for what was coming, what she was bringing on herself, what she was asking for, begging for. "Will you *really* pick up that ruler again . . . Daddy?"

Ya Allah, the Sheikh thought as he *leapt* to his feet and grabbed that wooden ruler, standing back up and pacing around the proud American woman on her knees before him, buttocks raised for Daddy, eyes turned towards the King, pussy dripping for the Sheikh. It certainly does seem complicated to be a woman in today's America!

And as he brought that paddle down hard for a solid first strike that echoed off the classroom walls, the Sheikh reminded himself that it was perhaps equally complicated being a King in today's Arabia.

20

"It is not that complicated, Zareena. I am a king, and she will submit to my will. Eventually."

Zareena raised an eyebrow and looked her husband up and down as the Sheikh paced through the living room of the hotel suite.

"Your will? Is that what you call it?" she asked. "Well, at least you have re-submitted to the custom of wearing pants in public buildings."

The Sheikh frowned, his green eyes narrowing as his brown face darkened with color. "Ya Allah, Habib's people . . . you have photographs?"

Zareena *screeched* with laughter, closing her eyes

Surrogate for the Sheikh

and waving him off. "Oh, *please!* I am just pushing you, Dhom! It is OK. It is all right. Have your fun. Enjoy her. Allah knows you deserve something with a woman who is not being paid to fuck you."

The Sheikh's jaw tightened at the remark, and he narrowed his eyes at Zareena before letting it pass. "She will be paid to carry my child—if you have your way, Zareena."

"If *we* have *our* way, Dhom," Zareena said, holding her voice steady.

"I have changed my mind, and my way is now different," Dhom said, his steadiness matching hers as he stopped his pacing and stood with arms folded, looking down at where Zareena lounged on the blue sofa, her black hijab spread like dark wings across the cushion.

"Yes, you told me," she said, looking away and then back up at him. "You will get this woman to agree to be your wife without a wedding, your spouse without marriage. She will live in the shadows like my faithful Alma. To the world she will be a hired surrogate who now just happens to live in her own chambers in the Royal Palace of Mizra. She will raise her child. Bear more children with you. We will all be one happy family. Ya Allah, some magical condition has somehow replaced your brain with one dumb penis and two clueless testicles. It is a medical miracle."

"Mock me if you want, Zareena," the Sheikh said,

unmoved and unfazed. "But you do not know this woman like I do."

"I know what it *means* to be a woman," Zareena spat as she looked up at him. "And I will tell you that *no* woman—certainly not *this* woman—is going to agree to an arrangement like this."

"You do not know that."

"By God, Dhom. OK. You have asked her this already, yes?"

"Yes."

"And she has said what?"

The Sheikh hesitated and rubbed his stubble. "She will need some time."

Zareena laughed up at him and shook her head. "So wise. So powerful. And so dumb!" she cried.

"Excuse me? Zareena, your tone is unacc—"

"Oh, please. Don't shush me when I am trying to stop you from walking head first into a trap. Dhom, this woman is smart and strong, and—"

"She is honest and she is good. She just needs time."

"Of course she is honest and good. I would only choose a woman of the strongest character, the deepest resiliency, the best of her breed. But she is still a *woman*! She cannot out-think her own biology, her own psychology, her own *destiny*!"

"*I* am her destiny!" the Sheikh roared now, spreading his arms out wide and turning away from the Sheikha as he began to furiously pace again.

"Then tell her the truth," Zareena said sweetly, eyes

wide and innocent. "Tell her of every detail. In fact I can tell her, since I know more of the details. Shall we call for the limousine? We can meet her outside the school itself!"

The Sheikh continued to pace, his fists clenching, jaw tightening as if he was holding himself back from saying something he might regret. By God, he is taken by this woman, Zareena thought as she watched her husband pace and rub his jaw, the tension surging through him in the most, the most . . . *endearing* way!

"Oh, Dhom," she said as a tear formed at the corner of her left eye. "I yearn to see you happy with a woman, in love with a woman, at peace with a woman, a child, a family. As much as I speak of a woman's biology, a woman's needs, a woman's physical destiny, I know the same needs exist deep in a man's soul as well. But we chose this path as much as this path chose us, my King. You know it as well as I do, but you are clouded by the needs of your mortality, the longings of your biology, the instinct to claim your mate and raise your flock. That need is real and good, pure and true. But we are not normal people. We do not have the luxury of retiring to private family life. We live in public. We live *for* the public."

The Sheikh turned now, his eyes misty, handsome face twisted in anguish. Zareena could see the torment, sense the conflict, feel how the emotion was tearing this stoic beast of a man in two.

But he is still proud and willful, stubborn and immovable, she reminded herself. And sadly, the woman he has chosen—the woman we *both* have chosen—is also proud and stubborn. She may fall in love with him. She may bear his child. She may give herself to him again and again. But without the certainty of that marriage bond, the most human of symbols, she will eventually leave him. She will leave him even if she does not want to leave him. She may not even understand why she does it, but it will happen. Perhaps not in a year. Perhaps not in five years. But it is inevitable. No proud woman can stay true to herself being a mistress in the shadows. She will leave him.

And she will take the child with her.

Now Zareena's tears evaporated into the dry air, and she was that stoic queen again, the woman who had made the hardest of choices and would continue to make the hardest of choices.

"OK, Dhom," she said to him now. "She needs time, you say. And you have asked her to accompany you to Mizra, yes?"

The Sheikh nodded. "Yes, but it is too much, too soon for her. She speaks of the job. Lease on her apartment. Something else I cannot remember. All of it easily done away with, in my opinion. But yet—"

Zareena took a breath now. "What does she know of me, Dhom?"

Dhomaar blinked and stopped pacing. "She knows . . . very little. I have only told her of . . . of . . ."

"You have told her that our marriage is an illusion. That we are not romantic or sexual partners, though we are indeed partners for life, like it or not."

The Sheikh swallowed and nodded.

Zareena nodded, sitting up and crossing her legs on the sofa. "So here is what we do, my king. Here is how you can have it all. Now, you do not want Grace to ever find out that she was selected to be our surrogate. Correct?"

The Sheikh looked past her and then slowly nodded.

"So we will never speak of it. She will never know of it. Here is what I am willing to do for you, my Sheikh. Listen carefully."

21

The Sheikh exhaled and smiled as he entered his private suite and collapsed onto the king-sized bed as Zareena's plan swirled through his head.

Ya Allah, he thought. After all these years it is so hard to know what part is real and what is the act, is it not? No matter. Our motives are true, even if the methods are twisted. And of course, as Zareena says, the universe is there behind the scenes, its creatures and coincidences guiding us. So as twisted as the methods may be, perhaps we will get to the right place, the place where destiny lives.

Three weeks, the Sheikh thought as he relaxed and

reminded himself to enjoy the next few days just "getting to know" this woman who had stumbled into his life in her red dress, complicating things in the most wonderful, whimsical, *worrisome* way.

Three weeks, he thought. Three weeks, and then it begins.

22

Three weeks, Gracie told herself as she eyed that unopened pregnancy kit in her medicine cabinet. I'll wait three weeks before opening that horrendously pink box and finding out if my life is going to change.

She touched the box and then closed the cabinet, walking out into the living room of her one-bedroom apartment in South Tulsa. God, her life had *already* changed, hadn't it? It had been almost seventeen days with the Sheikh now. Seventeen *incredible* days. With a Sheikh. A married Sheikh. A married Sheikh who insisted his wife knew about them and didn't care because their marriage was a sham. A married Sheikh in a fake marriage who insisted Grace was pregnant with his child. And who wanted Grace to *move* to some *island kingdom* and be his ... sorta kinda wife whom he could never ever actually marry. Was that complicated enough for a woman in today's America?! Was that complicated enough to check herself into the goddamn *psych ward* so she could be studied for clues as to why she wasn't *dead* from anxiety and insanity?!

Now Gracie frowned away the smile of disbelief and excitement that had been more or less plastered on her face all day these past couple of weeks. She frowned because in her little mental recap of the lesson plan—or rather her life plan from the last two weeks—it seemed like something was missing. Because in all their conversations, the Sheikh had been fairly sketchy about exactly how much Zareena knew. Yes, Dhom told Grace point-blank that Zareena knew about them. But when Gracie asked him the other day about how she'd feel about her having his child, Dhom waved her off, saying they should wait until she knew she was pregnant.

Now *that* was strange, wasn't it? After all, it was Dhom who insisted that he had knocked her up that very first night. And God, now she believed it. She really did! So now he was all "scientific" about it when it came to telling his ... his *wife* about it? God, it sounded so stupid when she thought it through, didn't it? Like what kind of a *moron* just takes some billionaire's word that his wife's a lesbian and she'll be cool with him knocking some other chick up and then bringing her to live with them? Seriously, if a woman told Gracie that, Grace would call them (in her own mind only, of course . . .) a dumb bimbo who gives all women a bad name!

And now as Grace sat there alone in her apartment, some of the manic haze of the magical whirlwind of love and sex that Dhom had spun her up into subsiding, she felt a distant paranoia creep its way in, a feeling like something was off, that she wasn't seeing the big picture. After all, what wife—lesbian or not—is going to be cool with a husband having a child with someone else? Unless the other woman was a surrogate, of course. And of course you don't go and stick your *cock* into a surrogate, do you?

Do you? came the paranoid thought as Grace frowned and touched her stomach. After all, these people were royalty from halfway around the world. They didn't have children. No heir. Grace had felt weird about asking why, even though she wanted to ask. But she had thought that hey, she already knew Zareena and Dhom didn't have kids. That was public knowledge. The rest of it wasn't her business.

Um, yeah, it's your business if you're pregnant, she thought now as that paranoia grew larger and larger, a sickening feeling taking over as it dawned on her that here was a king and queen with no heirs, the king seducing some random woman at what was probably a very conducive time in her cycle. And then the queen seems *totally* chilled about it while the king just hangs out with that random woman, "getting to know her" as he keeps fucking her even while insisting she's already pregnant?

Am I being played, she wondered now as she quickly sat down on the bed and put her head in her hands. I know *nothing* about this family, *nothing* about his wife, so little about *him*! And I'm getting swept up in his whirlwind of seduction, the insane sex, the expensive dinners, this crazy talk of me living with him and our children in his palace.

None of it made sense, of course. And Gracie wanted to cry one moment and laugh the next. It felt like a fairy tale one moment, a horror movie the next. She was convinced he loved her one moment and sure he was playing her the next. She was a proud new mother in the dream, the discarded surrogate in the nightmare.

Finally she couldn't handle it. She just could not. It had to stop. And there was one way it *would* stop. One test that would sort it all out, bring some calm into the chaos, give her some room to fucking *breathe*!

So even though it was just day seventeen and it might be too early, she stormed to the bathroom and ripped open that atrocious pink packaging and pulled out three sticks and took off her panties and peed on the sticks and waited. She waited and stared, looking at the timer on her phone.

Shit, I can't look, she thought, suddenly closing her eyes and turning away. But she had to look, and when she looked she saw that all of those sticks now had the heads of pixies and goblins and trolls, and they were all squealing and yelling, pointing and howling, screeching and hooting as they plucked at her boobs and poked at her belly and laughed at her fat face and called her a pregnant princess, a knocked-up queen, a stupid bitch whose life had just gotten very, very complicated.

She dropped those sticks and walked out of the bathroom in a dizzying haze, frowning as she thought she heard a sound by the fire escape in the kitchen. Mice? So now I'm a dumb bimbo who's pregnant. And I have mice in my kitchen. What next? Alien abduction?

And as she frowned at that strange noise once again, she felt a presence behind her, and before she could scream a black hood came down over her head, a needle slid into her soft arm, and those green-eyed aliens held hands with the pregnancy-pixies and they all danced an Irish jig in the swirling dreamscape of Gracie Garner's nightmare.

23
<u>FIRST MONTH</u>

"Do not be ridiculous. You have to eat. You have been here three days and you have not eaten. You will starve to death, you foolish woman!"

Gracie Garner stared at Queen Zareena across the large teakwood table in the day-room of the Southern Wing of Mizra's Royal Palace. These sprawling, lavish rooms with pink sandstone walls and sandbrushed marble floors had been the setting for Gracie's golden nightmare of the past three days, and she stared blankly at the tall, thin woman in the black hijab and the sequined veil which was now hanging down and away from her face.

She's pretty, Gracie thought. This was the first time she had actually seen Zareena's face clearly, and the olive-skinned woman had beautiful high cheekbones underlining deep-set eyes that seemed to be the color of dark sand. Hollow, sunken cheeks though, like this woman didn't eat very much herself.

"I won't starve to death because the goddamn Navy Seals are going to parachute in here and kill your medieval asses. Then I'll eat a Snickers bar on the plane-ride home, thank you very much," Gracie said. She was lightheaded and woozy, though she had in fact eaten a few pieces of fruit from the heavy, gold-plated bowls that were all over her chambers. She'd also snacked on some nuts, dates, and kefir, along with drinking tons of water and a fair amount of sickeningly sweet tea that she was kinda addicted to now.

"You and your Navy Seals and Snickers bars," Zareena muttered. "They will not come, because nobody knows you are here. Now please eat some warm food, and then we can begin."

"Begin what?" Gracie said with a frown. She'd been here three days, two of which were a whirlwind of recovering from whatever the hell drug had knocked her out. Then jet lag, paranoia, anger, fear, thoughts of suicide, fantasies of murder, more anger, some indignation, a bit of self-pity, some despair, and now, thankfully, straight-up sulkiness.

"The vetting process," Zareena said, looking at her nails and then back up at Gracie.

Surrogate for the Sheikh

"Who's vetting what?" Gracie said, that frown digging deeper.

"I am vetting you. What do you think?"

"What do I think? I think you are insane and unhinged, as is your husband. Who is where, by the way?"

"The Sheikh has agreed to stay away for a period of one month," said Zareena.

"Ah. So this mysterious vetting process is going to take one month?"

Zareena shrugged. "Could be shorter. Probably longer. A lot depends on you."

Gracie sighed now, glancing at the bowl of steaming vegetable rice pilaf and the fragrant spiced lentils to the left. There was fresh pita bread, hummus, some kind of lamb dish, and . . . OK, stop. We are on a hunger strike!

"Depends on me? And how is that?" Gracie said.

Zareena leaned forward on the table now, pushing the succulent pilaf closer to Gracie to where aroma of saffron spice almost made her swoon.

"OK, Ms. Garner," said Zareena firmly. "Here it is for you, in plain English. My husband has kept me abreast of his affair with you. He has told me of his intentions. And he—"

"His *intentions*? Which are what, may I ask? I mean, I'd ask *him*, but—"

"Allow me to finish, and then you may rant," Zareena said with a steadiness that made Gracie actually want to shut up and listen. "My husband cares for you, and I believe you care for him. At least he believes you care for him, and I see no reason to question that belief."

Gracie blinked and looked down at her hands as the queen continued.

"Dhomaar tells me you are aware of our personal marriage situation. Yes?"

Gracie nodded silently.

"Good," said Zareena. "So you understand that I am . . . I am *delighted* that Dhomaar has found the woman with whom he wants to spend the rest of his life."

"The rest of his life. He said that?" Gracie said softly, wondering if that tingle was hunger or something else.

"He has said it to you as well, has he not?" Zareena asked matter-of-factly.

"Well, not quite like that," Gracie started to say. "OK, yes."

"And do you feel that way about him?"

Gracie frowned. "I mean . . . um . . . it's kinda hard to answer that now that I've been, you know, *kidnapped* by his *wife*. With his knowledge, it appears! That sorta kinda might change things, don't you think, you psychotic, fanatical, *witch*!"

Zareena sighed and slammed her palms on the table, pushing herself to her feet. "As I said, how long this vetting process takes depends on you. But if for a moment you think I will accept a woman into my royal family, to raise a child who will be heir to the kingdom of my ancestors, to be the lifelong consort and partner to my husband and cousin, a man I care for deeply and truly . . . yes, if you believe that I will succumb to your sulking and ranting, your threats of Navy Seals and firebombing, your weak attempts at inducing guilt, and your pathetic display of a hunger strike, then you are not the smart and strong, practical and sensible, stable and serene woman my husband says he is in love with. I *will* vet you before accepting you into this home. And you *will* treat me like I am the goddamn Queen."

She stood there and crossed her arms over her chest and looked down at Gracie. But Gracie slumped in her wooden chair and crossed *her* arms over *her* chest and looked up at Zareena.

They held eye contact as the sun moved across the desert sky, and finally Zareena exhaled and nodded.

"Very well. I will return at the end of the month. There will be attendants at your beck and call, medical staff if you need it. And the Southern Wing of the Royal Palace has over thirty rooms and chambers, gymnasia and entertainment centers, indoor gardens and outdoor fountains within the palace walls. You are a prisoner here, make no mistake. But you cannot say that I am placing any physical hardship upon you. As for mental hardship . . . well, Ms. Grace Garner. You will have one month of solitude to ponder the truism that at least some of your mental state is *your* responsibility—kidnap victim or not. Good day, Ms. Garner."

Zareena snapped her fingers as three hijab-clad attendants walked out through the large double-doors leading to the central dome of the palace, and now Grace was alone. Alone with a lot of very good-looking food, and a strange feeling of . . . of . . . never mind. She wasn't going to give in. She could out-sulk anyone, even a goddamn queen!

We'll see who blinks first, she thought as she looked around and slowly let her fingers crawl towards the warm pita bread.

Those double-doors opened now, and Gracie pulled her hand back and crossed her arms over her chest again. It was just an attendant with a small tray, and Gracie looked up at the veiled woman and raised an eyebrow.

"Yes?" Gracie asked.

The attendant placed the tray on the table, bowed, and backed out of the room, and Gracie *almost* broke a smile when she looked down and saw a gold-rimmed plate, in the center of which was a very nice arrangement of three double-sized Snickers bars.

24
__SECOND MONTH__

Zareena looked at herself in the gold-rimmed mirror of her private chambers in the Eastern Wing, and she sighed and shook her head at her reflection.

"If this were a fairy tale, I would be the evil stepmother," she muttered as she leaned forward and carefully applied her standard black eyeliner.

Not any more though, she told herself with a smile that was part happiness part surprise. It had been almost two months now, and Grace Garner had . . . well, she had impressed the Queen. The woman has something, Zareena had told herself when the first month passed and word came round that Gracie was eating fine and appeared happy or at the very least not particularly depressed or even lonely.

That had been the first sign alerting Zareena to the inner strength of this woman: the ability to handle solitude—especially under duress. After all, as Zareena had made clear to Gracie over the course of their lengthy discussions in the second month (when Grace had decided it was time to talk . . .), Grace was being vetted not just for suitability to be her husband's "consort" or "secret wife" or whatever they chose to call the arrangement, but Grace was being vetted for a situation where she might actually become Queen!

"You're kidding," Gracie had said just two days ago, when Zareena had felt comfortable enough—and *close* enough—with the woman to express the unlikely but possible situation.

Zareena had shrugged, smiling mischievously as she took a seedless date from the plate between the two women. "I should not be telling you this because it gives you incentive to poison me in my sleep, but yes. If I am to pass—whether tomorrow or in fifty years—then Dhom will be free to take a wife. And that wife will be Queen. So yes, Grace. You should know this."

"Oh, God," Grace had said, touching her neck and then squeezing Zareena's arm with a warmth that had sent a tingle through the queen in the most uncomfortable of ways. "Oh, God, I'm so humbled. I can't even believe we're talking about this. I can't even believe—"

"I cannot either," Zareena had said, looking down at the way Grace's tender white hand lay draped over the Queen's slender brown forearm. "It is a testament to you. I did not expect . . . I did not expect to be talking about such things with you, Grace."

Gracie had frowned. "What do you mean? I thought you had this vetting process all planned out. Like bulleted lists. I'm surprised there isn't a Powerpoint. Or is there?"

Zareena had smiled and drawn her arm away, cognizant of Alma's presence in the background of the large open courtyard between the Southern and Eastern wings, where they could see the domes of the palace rising up into the diamond-studded night sky of the Mizrahi desert.

"Listen, Grace," Zareena had said. "I am truly taken by surprise by how we have connected. I mean, I was of course aware of your intelligence, your psychological profile, your—"

"My what?" Grace had said, frowning and snorting. "You been reading my Facebook quizzes?"

"You have no idea," Zareena muttered, blinking and swallowing hard as she prepared to come clean. She had wondered for a moment if she was perhaps getting played by Grace—Zareena the master-manipulator getting out-manipulated by the disarming straightforwardness of this curiously strong schoolteacher from Oklahoma. But Zareena quickly overruled that part of her because it just felt . . . it felt *right* to do so! The queen had been led this far by what *felt* right, what *felt* like the universe's way, what *felt* like the twisted pathway to their shared destinies: hers, Dhom's, Gracie's, and of the kingdom that was bringing them together.

So Zareena looked up at the heavens and took a breath and swallowed hard once more. Then she talked.

She talked about salted oases and signs from the universe, failed attempts at getting pregnant, and her beliefs about the female body. She talked about searching for surrogates, and tracking the menstrual cycles of American women. She talked of the purity of her own beliefs, and acknowledged the twisted madness in how they played out. Most of all, she talked of Dhom not knowing about Grace until the two first met in the Grand Ballroom, that the first meeting was a set up but still real. Supremely real. After all, that was the point of it all!

"It *was* real," Zareena said, desperately searching Grace's eyes for some sign that this woman could handle the twisted truth. "You and Dhom *are* real. I swear it."

"I know," said Gracie, her eyes firm, her voice steady, her back straight. "I know."

"Of course," Zareena had said, first in relief, but then cocking her head at how calm Grace seemed. "Of course you know Dhom and you are the real thing. Of course. You must feel it when you are with him. You must sense it in every touch, every kiss, every embrace. You must—"

"Yes, I know what we have is real, even though how we got to it was through a deception," Gracie said, reaching for the queen's arm in the darkness again, squeezing tight, holding on as Zareena blinked in embarrassment at the tingle she was certain Grace would pick up. "But I also know about the rest. Well, I mean, I didn't know I was being tracked and monitored and . . . and how they hell does anyone track a woman's cycle? Shit, even I barely know when Aunt Flo's gonna pop in this month!"

"I do not understand," Zareena had said quietly, moving her arm away and placing it down at her side.

"What? The Aunt Flo thing, or . . ."

"Do not mock me," Zareena said. "I can still have you beheaded and fed to the camels."

Grace had laughed and clapped her hands before going serious and leaning forward on the small table in the rapidly darkening courtyard. "I may have been kinda dumb in all this, but I'm not *that* dumb. I mean, it took me a few weeks to put it together. But come on: Royal family. No kids. No heir. Dhomaar always muttering about filling me with his seed. Putting the best of him in me. Ovulation. Clearly he was out to make a kid."

Zareena had frowned. "And you are . . . you are not

upset? Not offended? Not going to rant and sulk, call for firebombs and Navy Seals?"

Gracie took a breath and shrugged. "Well, perhaps it hasn't completely sunk in, or maybe it's the past two months of this weird dream I've stepped into. So with the caveat that I *absolutely* reserve the right to a future rant and perhaps a firebomb, the truth right now is . . . is that given where things seem to be heading, I'm sorta at peace with how things started." She shrugged. "I know I *want* to be angrier. But for some reason I'm not. I guess . . . I guess it's just kinda complicated being a woman in today's America. The bottom line is that people meet and fall in love in all kinds of messed up, twisted, ridiculous ways. There's arranged marriages happening in the U.S. all the time. There's other weird matchmaking that I don't want to *think* about. You said it earlier: What Dhom and I shared is real, and it was real from the first meeting. God, Zareena, you made *sure* the first meeting would be real! Maybe you didn't expect it to play out exactly this way, but you were our matchmaker! Twisted, sick, loony, and certifiably *mad*. But shit, what a story for the kids!"

Zareena had *squealed* with relieved laughter, almost bursting into tears as she laughed again and reached out, caressing Gracie's smooth round cheek with an affection that Grace didn't seem to mind. They shared a long moment of silent connection, with the stars watching, the moon sighing, the palm trees bearing silent witness. Then finally Zareena pulled back and stood to leave.

"Trust me," said the queen. "If you think womanhood in today's America is complicated, try being a lesbian in yesterday's Arabia."

25
THIRD MONTH

"Firstly, she is not a lesbian. Secondly, I am committed to you and you alone. And thirdly," said Zareena as she turned and looked sternly at the seething Alma. "Thirdly, I am Queen, and I do not have to explain myself to anyone."

"Are you my queen when you put your face between my legs and slide your tongue into my forbidden slit," Alma snapped. "When you spread my buttocks and push your royal fingers into—"

"Enough!" Zareena shouted, her dark face going red. "I will not hear this. You are mad if you think there is a need to be jealous! I have not touched another woman in twenty years!" She swallowed now, taking a breath as she narrowed her eyes at the shivering Alma. "But as I said, I am Queen, and I do not need to explain myself to anyone. *Anyone!*"

Alma bowed her head and stepped back. But before leaving the room she stopped and turned. "In other words, there is a need to be jealous."

"I sleep alone tonight," said the Queen, holding in her rage that was fueled by just a nagging little bit of . . . guilt. "Do not return to my presence until I call for you."

Alma paused as if shocked. Then she bowed again and left without another word.

Zareena sighed as she pulled her hijab off over her head and let it drop onto the hand-woven Persian rug by her massive old bed. A part of her understood Alma's feelings. But Alma had her place, and this was the lay of the land. All of them carried the burden of their royal lives—attendants included. Lovers included. Alma would get over it soon enough.

Now the Queen's mind drifted back to Grace Garner. Dhom had arrived in Mizra at the beginning of this third month, and from all outward signs their reunion had been electric, ecstatic, scandalously loud to the point where the Queen had hurriedly replaced the Southern Wing's attendants with her most trusted insiders to keep the rumors to a minimum.

Of course, the rumors would only rise and spread as Grace began to show. And as Grace began to be seen more around the palace. Although Grace was still technically confined to the Southern Wing, it was clear that soon she would have the run of the palace—now that the Sheikh was back and all seemed well in the world.

Ya Allah, how the universe continues to surprise me, Zareena thought as she rolled her beige panties down her slim thighs and walked to her large teakwood dresser near the bed. To think I truly allowed myself to believe that if the discussions with Grace had gone in a different direction, that if Grace had laughed at the suggestion of living here unmarried with Dhom to raise a child with him and his lesbian-cousin wife . . . yes, I was prepared to take the child by any means necessary. Blackmail. Coercion. Manipulation. Torture? Hah! By God, I *was* the evil stepmother!

And Snow White has won me over, has she not, Zareena thought as she pulled open the top drawer and reached inside, her pussy tightening as she reached for the thin satin cloth she had hidden away back there . . . hidden away after finding it crumpled up in Dhomaar's tuxedo jacket—the one he wore to the Grand Ballroom, the night it all began.

Zareena pushed away the thought that she was a filthy, twisted woman as she brought out those ripped

Surrogate for the Sheikh

black panties which Gracie had worn beneath her red dress that night. She held them up to the light, her left hand dropping down to her crotch as she breathed deep of that woman's feminine smell.

"Oh, God," she muttered, touching her clit and backing away to the bed. She heard a sound outside her curtain now, turning to look but then thinking it was just a breeze.

"Alma?" she called out in a panic. But there was no answer, and so the Queen pulled the curtain aside and checked. No one. No one but the queen and her fantasies.

26
FOURTH MONTH

If this had started as a dream and turned into a nightmare, it was now a fantasy, Gracie thought as she pushed herself up off the Sheikh, who had sat her down on his cock three times today alone, making her ride him to orgasm carefully and slowly, now that she was showing a little of that baby bump.

Dhomaar had returned almost two months ago, and now she could say for sure that they knew each other's favorite colors.

"OK, it is purple," she told him when he pointed out that she did not seem to like green as much as she had led him to believe. "I just didn't want you to think you could figure me out so quick."

"Trust me," Dhom said. "It will take a while to figure you out. And by God, I am looking forward to it."

"Well, you've got five months before you're gonna be on diaper-duty, so if you got some questions, then now's the time, buddy."

"The heir to the kingdom of Mizra will not need diapers. He will just come and go as he pleases. Wherever he pleases."

"Eww," she said, twisting her face and pushing him away.

He shrugged. "You will have to learn a few of the customs of this savage land, my lady. Now that I think about it," he added, looking at his cock, which seemed ready to get hard again—for the fourth time that day. "It is time for today's lesson."

"Oh, trust me, I don't need a lesson in diapers or lack thereof."

"That is not the savage custom I speak of," he said quietly, walking to the hand-carved cabinet of dark wood that sat against the pink sandstone walls. He opened it and pulled out something that looked . . . looked . . .

"What. The. Fu—"

"Camel leather," said the Sheikh, holding up the ominous looking whip, long brown strands of sun-cured rawhide hanging down, hundreds of little tassels with rounded studs at each end. "Come. We will start easy. We have the entire month to break this in. To break you in."

"Um, what happens next month," she said, covering her naked buttocks with her hands as she walked over to him, squinting in terrified curiosity at that camel-leather *thing* in the Sheikh's hands.

Now the Sheikh pulled open both doors of the long dark cabinet, and Gracie's buttocks seized up as she stared at the rows upon rows of . . .

"That's a lot to learn in five months," she whispered as she felt her pussy start to ooze in urgent anticipation. "We'd better get started, don't you think?"

27
FIFTH MONTH

"We have already started. Grace is a quick learner. Smart as a whip."

Zareena frowned at Dhomaar before winking and nodding. "We are still talking about Arabic lessons, yes?"

The Sheikh grinned and shrugged as he put on his sunglasses and walked back to the silver Range Rover. He took a long drink of the lime juice waiting on a golden tray, slamming the glass down on the hood of the car as an attendant swooped in to grab it.

Dhomaar walked past the queen again, all the way

to the edge of the small oasis that had been on its way to a salty death just a year ago. He reached down and scooped up some of the clear blue water in his palm, tasting it and then turning to the queen.

"I suppose this is an omen that things are back to following the path of destiny," Dhomaar said, trying to roll his eyes but finding it hard to do so after tasting the fresh and sweet water of the desert he loved. "Whereas our surveyors assure me there is a scientific explanation. Something to do with rainfall patterns and date palm roots."

"Scientific explanation," Zareena said with a smirk. "OK, so what is the scientific explanation for the blind old Sheikh of Kalyan seemingly backing down from his dreams of conquest and invasion?"

Dhom snorted. "The scientific explanation is that the whole invasion thing was unscientific to begin with! A blind madman is overhead talking to himself, and we are to take his rants seriously!"

"Blind madmen are notoriously and scientifically unpredictable," Zareena said. "In such a case, paranoia is the sensible option for the circumspect ruler. At any rate, if the Sheikh of Kalyan was never serious, perhaps that is even more of an indication that the universe has its ways of influence and coercion. Without the warnings that came through Alma, we may never have started down this path. You and Grace may never have met."

"We would have met some other way," Dhom started to say, and then he caught himself when he realized Zareena had trapped him into saying something suspiciously close to the unscientific statement that he and Grace were inevitable, meant to be, that it was fate, destiny, goddamn *magic*!

He grinned and looked away when he saw Zareena's expression of triumph, and he tried very hard not to reward her with some sign that by God, sometimes he thought it did feel like magic!

Zareena finally looked at her phone and spoke. "Well, speaking of science, the Lamaze instructor will be waiting for you and Grace. The woman charges nine hundred an hour."

"I would pay her nine thousand an hour *not* to come," Dhomaar muttered as he got into the Range Rover and snapped his fingers for a cup of sweet tea.

"Ah, you love it," Zareena whispered. "I have seen you with her in those sessions. It is beautiful to watch, my husband. It warms my heart."

Dhomaar looked over and frowned. "You have watched us in those sessions? When?"

Zareena quickly blinked and looked away. "Oh, I just happened to be walking by and I stopped to see my fake husband getting ready to be a *real* husband."

"Ah, because she is a real woman, my Grace," Dhom muttered, smiling as he thought of how insanely hot her curves were with the added heft of the pregnancy. He could barely keep his hands off her, and in fact part of his discomfort with the Lamaze sessions was that he was painfully erect about halfway into them! All he wanted was that damned instructor to get the hell out so he could strip those clothes off his curvy baby-mama and take her right there on the damned yoga mats, in front of the mirror of that exercise room!

Well, not if Zareena was going to be watching from the shadows, Dhom thought as he glanced over at his wife now, looking down at her slender frame, petite breasts, boyish bob-cut beneath the hood of her black gown. Alma was a slender woman too, it occurred to Dhom as the car raced silently through the desert, the curves of those rolling dunes gliding by as Dhom tried to push away the thoughts that seemed to be popping into his mind suddenly.

"Why don't you join us for the Lamaze one day," he said quietly now, glancing at Zareena and noticing how she flinched.

She snorted, glancing into his eyes with a questioning look. "Ah, no. I do not think—"

"Why not? We will all three of us have a hand in raising the child." He grinned now, shrugging and then reaching over and squeezing his wife's hand. "Just like all three of us had a hand in conceiving this child."

Her eyes teared up as she held his hand, and they rode in silence for the rest of the trip back.

"We shall see," Zareena said as they pulled into the palace driveway. "We shall see."

28
<u>SIXTH MONTH</u>

"**I** can't even see my toes, my belly's so big! I can't even see my belly, my boobs are so big!"

"Can you see this, my woman?"

"Oh, God, Dhom! What is that? And what are you going to do with . . . oh *God*, Dhom!"

29
SEVENTH MONTH

"**N**o Lamaze instructor today," Dhom said to her. "She fell off a camel."

"Oh, that's awful. Why was she riding a camel?" said Gracie as she took his arm to steady herself so she could waddle to the side of the exercise studio where they had their Lamaze sessions. One wall was all mirror, and Gracie looked at her enormous belly and bulging boobs in that loose white t-shirt that was the size of a sail. She wore black tights that could fit an elephant, she thought—though for some reason Dhom seemed to get only more insatiable as she got closer to full-on cow status. Perhaps he'd even be able to milk her soon! She'd actually felt some pressure building up behind her nipples—the areolas of which had grown as big as saucers, it seemed. She really did feel like a cow ready to be milked!

But she also felt beautiful, and she felt loved. By Dhom, of course. But also by everyone else, it seemed! She had grown to love her attendants, and now that she spoke a smattering of Arabic, people were literally falling at her feet from pride that this American woman was taking the trouble to learn their language. And there was Zareena, of course, with whom Grace felt a real bond, something more than friendship and not quite sisterhood. It was familial, yeah. But there was still some weird tension.

Well, of *course* there's weird tension. The situation is weird! Our family is going to be weird! What kind of a triangle are we? Hah!

"She was riding a camel because we are in the goddamn desert and it is a perfectly acceptable thing to ride a camel here," Dhom said.

"Huh? What? Oh, the Lamaze woman. OK, well, should we just head back to the Southern Wing? I've only lived here seven months, and there's at least five different indoor fountains I haven't seen yet."

"No," said Dhom. "Let us do it anyway. We do not need the instructor."

"Really? You want to do it anyway? That's so sweet."

"This is what is sweet," he growled as he reached around from behind her and pressed her right boob, squeezing and kneading as she backed up into him and rubbed her body against him.

"Oh, shit," she groaned as she felt her nipple stiffen up as he pinched it through the white cotton t-shirt. "Oh, *shit!*" she cried now when she felt the liquid ooze from her nipple as the Sheikh pinched that stiff nub and reached for the other boob.

"What is it?" he said, rubbing his cock against her ass in those black yoga pants.

"You don't feel it through the cloth?" she said when she realized what it was.

"Do you feel *this* through the cloth?" he growled as he pushed the peak of his erection between her buttcheeks and pulled her back against him as he ground and swirled, kneading her breasts harder, pinching both nipples so hard she could feel the lactate start to flow.

"I'm leaking," she giggled as she rubbed her ass against him.

"Of course you are," he muttered as he reached one hand down and cupped her beautiful pot-belly, now gently rubbing her crotch. "Of course you are leaking for Daddy. Just like Daddy is hard for—"

"No, not that," she said, frowning as she realized it felt damn good as the pressure behind her nipples got relieved as some of that milk got squeezed out.

"My boobs. Do that again. With my nipples. Yes, that. Oh, *God*, that feels good."

"Ya Allah, your nipples are wet through the cloth, Grace," said the Sheikh, frowning for a moment and then cocking his head. "Is it . . . is it your . . ."

"Hm hmmm," she muttered as he pressed her nipples, both at once, sending a wonderful tingle through her as she suddenly *yearned* to have those swollen peaks sucked and nibbled, pulled and plucked, squeezed and . . . milked.

"So soon?" he said as he started to bunch up the cloth of her shirt even as he kept squeezing those nipples.

"Seven months gone," she groaned as she arched her back and pulled her own t-shirt up over her head, feeling her arousal soar as she felt the sticky flow soaking her bra cup. "Oh, God, get this bra off me, Dhom."

"As you wish," he grunted as he slipped off the double-clasps and lifted the large reinforced cups off her swollen nipples, revealing her large, glistening areolas. "Oh, bloody hell, you are beautiful. Oh, my God, come here. Bring those here. Bring those to Daddy."

"Milk me first," she gasped as he tried to turn her and suck her nipples. "I want to see myself in milk for the first time. Then you can taste me. But I want you to milk me first."

"My God, yes, I will milk you," he muttered, helping

her to the floor, leaning her up against his hard body so they both faced that mirrored wall. "Ya Allah, you look so beautiful and full, flowing like the goddamn mother of the universe."

She giggled as he squeezed, and now she gasped as she looked at her reflection, how large she was, how perfect she was, how her breasts were flowing as her man milked her, squeezed her, poured her.

She closed her eyes and moaned as he squeezed her again, and now he was rubbing her crotch with one hand, licking her neck, still squeezing her nipple with increasing force.

"Does this feel good?" he muttered as he plucked at her nipple and pressed it back down hard, pumping her boob as her lactate flowed.

"Uh-huh," she muttered. "It feels good. I like being milked by Daddy."

"And Daddy likes milking his little girl when she's all pregnant and swollen, overflowing like the rivers after a rainstorm, the milk of life flowing down her breasts. She is mother to everyone now. Mother to the universe."

"The milk is for you right now, Daddy. Milk me for yourself now, Daddy," she groaned as she dropped her own hand down to her crotch, sliding her fingers into the waistband of her yoga pants as she leaned back into him, her eyes clamped shut, the strangest fantasy flowing into her mind, rivers of milk flowing from her breast, feeding the world, hungry mouths, grateful lips, plants and animals reaching for her, gods and goddesses suckling at her, husbands and wives, old and young, men and women, boys and girls. She was mother to all. Mother to the mother even. "Milk me for yourself now, Daddy. Milk me for Daddy."

"What about Mommy?" he murmured as he grasped both her breasts now as she slid two fingers into her own cunt and drove, her thumb furiously rubbing her clit as the Sheikh kept going with the fantasy. "Isn't there some milk for Mommy? Doesn't my good baby girl want to be milked for Mommy as well as Daddy?"

"Oh, yeah," she moaned. "My milk belongs to Daddy, so he can milk me for Mommy. He can milk me for anyone."

"Then Daddy will milk his little girl for Mommy," he whispered. "Because she deserves to taste you. She had a hand in creating you too. So come now. Here we go. Relax and flow. Flow for Mommy. Flow for Mommy."

Now she felt lips closing around her right nipple, gently at first, tongue teasing the stiff point, now slowly circling her nub, lapping now, harder, lips closing in, clamping down, tight, tighter, teeth tenderly pulling at the nipples, sucking now, sucking more, sucking hard, sucking long, sucking deep, drinking from her, drinking in her, swallowing, slurping, sucking again, other nipple now, someone still pinching the other breast, her own fingers driving hard into her pussy.

Grace's eyelids fluttered open and closed, and she caught glimpses of herself in the mirror, glimpses of the Sheikh holding her in his arms, glimpses of Zareena . . .

"Oh, *God!*" she gasped when she realized what was happening, and just as she said it she *came*, suddenly and *hard*, and Grace swore she *squirted* into her panties as she came, and ohgod she was still rubbing her clit, still driving into her cunt, still gasping and heaving as she watched the dark face of the Queen bobbing back and forth on her breast, sucking and swallowing, licking and slurping, and Grace didn't stop with the fingers, and she was still coming, still flowing, still being milked by Daddy, sucked by Mommy, more fingers in her panties now, three fingers in her cunt now, the Queen's fingers, long and slender, curling and intertwining with Grace's own fingers, and that climax whipped itself up into white foam, a creamy froth, and she came and she came and she came, in Daddy's arms, in Mommy's mouth, her milk for all, Grace the universal mother, Grace the mother goddess, Grace, Grace, Grace.

30
EIGHTH MONTH

Grace. Grace. *Grace*!

Alma stood by the entrance to the dark, musty chambers of Sheikh Kalyan's run-down old palace. She could have had this meeting a long time ago, but had never taken her old contact up on the offer to visit Kalyan until just now. Until she saw something she could never unsee. That sight of the king and queen and Grace, beautiful and pregnant, flowing like the goddess of life, driving Zareena into rapture even as Grace herself climaxed with a childlike innocence, the

Sheikh holding her in his strong arms, the Sheikha helping her to orgasm as she drank her milk.

That was several weeks ago, and nothing of the sort had happened again. Indeed, it appeared as if the three of them had chosen to never speak of it, to let that moment live as a moment to itself, a moment independent of any reality, a moment that could only occur once. But that one moment carried a unique emotional power that almost broke Alma as she watched from the curtains.

Yes, it almost broke Alma to see her queen, her consort, her lover in that heavenly, surreal embrace that seemed so much more than just sexual gratification. And that was what tore Alma to shreds inside: the knowledge that the potential would always be there, even if nothing ever happened again; that there was some sort of love between Zareena and Grace, even if it was not sexual or romantic love.

Of course, Alma would take her own life before harming the queen or the Sheikh. And for a while taking her own life seemed like the preferred option. But then, in a moment of indignant madness, a solution came to her wounded soul.

"One bullet," she told the blind old Sheikh of Kalyan as he chewed on his gnarled fingers, drooling from the side of his mouth but listening with intense focus. "One bullet can give you a last taste of glory, old

Sheikh. One bullet will give you an unprotected nation with no heir, a king and queen emotionally shattered, a people with no means to resist. One bullet to end the line and start the chaos in which you can seize control."

"Kill a child?" the old Sheikh rasped in the shadow of the setting sun.

"There is no child yet," Alma said. "She is still with child, and so the one bullet will end the line. One bullet will take two."

"One bullet will take two," the Sheikh of Kalyan repeated, pointing two fingers off to the left of Alma. "One bullet will take two."

31
NINTH MONTH

"Well, I *have* been eating for two for a while now," Grace said as she waddled herself off the large weighing scale outside the third floor bathroom in the Southern Wing that had started off as her prison and was now going to be her lifelong home. "But still, this is ridiculous. I don't think I'd be allowed on an airplane, because it would just tip over to one side!"

"I do not understand why you are even weighing yourself," the Sheikh said as he helped her walk towards the day-room that opened up into a sprawling verandah which offered a beautiful view of the southern part of Mizra's capital city, with the massive white dome and four high minaret-towers of the grand public mosque occupying prime position.

"You should not even be walking," Zareena said, standing with arms folded across her chest. "Ya Allah, help her, Dhom! Get her to that sofa so she does not strain her knees! Do you know knee-injuries are extremely common during late-stage pregnancy?"

"So even Zareena thinks I'm a whale whose legs are going to snap from the sheer bulk," Grace said, rolling her eyes and then winking at Zareena in a way that made the queen smile.

Grace was due any day now. They could have scheduled a date and time and done a C-section, but Grace had said nothing doing, that her hips were plenty wide enough and besides, she sorta wanted the experience. Zareena's heart had jumped when Grace told her that she wanted to give birth in the palace, in the Southern Wing of the Palace, with midwives and medics present, of course—but also with the Sheikh and Sheikha there to witness the birth. If they wanted, of course.

"Of course I will be there if you will allow it," Zareena had said when Grace told her. "Ya Allah, I am honored to—"

"Oh, please," Grace had said, clearly fighting back tears. "I know you can still have me beheaded and fed to the camels."

"If she does that, I will eat those camels and then give birth to you myself and then get you pregnant again," Dhom had declared.

"Um, I don't think that came out right," Grace had said, staring wide-eyed at Dhom as Zareena doubled up and clapped her hands.

They had all laughed, the three of them, and the mood had been light and airy, joyful and optimistic. They truly felt like a family, Zareena had thought at the time. And it felt even more like a family now, she thought as she watched her fake-husband help his pregnant secret-wife/mistress/whatever-the-hell towards the green day-bed facing the verandah that overlooked the public gardens and the minarets of the Great Mosque of Mizra.

"Why do you not come and take some sun, my lady," came a sweetly accented voice from the queen's left, and Zareena frowned in surprise when she saw it was Alma.

She and Alma had long since made up—though there was still some kind of tension the queen picked up when the two were alone. She had dismissed it, chalking it up to her own guilt—even though Zareena did not truly believe she had cheated on Alma. That one time was ... something else. From another world. A bleedthrough from an alternate existence, perhaps.

"Were you looking for me, Alma?" the queen asked now, still frowning as she looked at her attendant, who did not venture far from Zareena's private chambers. "Is there a matter that needs my attention?"

"No, my Sheikha," said Alma. "I was just . . . I simply came to offer Ms. Garner my wishes."

"Ah, the palace rumor-mill has been churning it out," said Dhom, grinning as he glanced at Alma and then back at Grace. "Well, Lady Garner. Why don't you sit on your royal day-bed and receive the well-wishers."

Grace stopped and looked over at Alma and then the open verandah. "Actually, I think I'll take Alma's suggestion and get some sun. God knows I'm pale as an albino in winter, and once this little whale-baby gets popped out, who knows how much time I'll get to just lounge around in the sun."

"Allow me," said Alma, smiling and stepping between Dhom and Grace, taking Grace's arm and leading her out to the open balcony.

Zareena watched Alma and Grace, and she felt a strange chill come over her as the warm afternoon breeze swirled around her naked ankles, now curling its way up her hijab like tentacles, the arms of an octopus, the coils of a snake, every scale and suction cup whispering to the queen, that breeze itself tugging at the queen's gown.

"Alma?" Zareena said, taking a step towards the verandah as Grace stood there front and center even as Alma took an awkward step to the side, distanc-

Surrogate for the Sheikh

ing herself from Grace, it seemed. "Alma, may I have a word?"

Alma did not acknowledge the queen, though Zareena knew she had heard. Now that chill rose up to where it felt like she was being choked, pulled along by an invisible grip around her very neck, and the queen stepped out onto that balcony, another step now, a third step, now stepping out in front of Gracie Garner and stopping there as that desert breeze whispered again, a whisper that had started as a warning and was now a farewell, a thank you, a goodbye.

Things slowed down for the queen now, like time had stopped and everything was just a series of frames. She saw Alma mouth the words *No, my Queen*. She saw Alma look towards that high minaret in the distance. Now Alma leaping in front of the queen as the shot rang out, a single shot, a single bullet, slicing through space and time, taking Alma through the neck, bursting her jugular, crashing into Zareena's heart, stopping that magnificent heart, the heart of a queen, the heart of a woman, the only heart strong enough to stop that bullet from going any farther.

32
<u>ONE YEAR LATER</u>
<u>A WEDDING, A CORONATION,</u>
<u>A BABY SHOWER</u>

"First the wedding. Then my coronation. And we end the evening with the baby shower," Grace said firmly, writing out the schedule for the third time that day even as she adjusted the feeding cushion around her and switched Baby Dhom from her left nipple to her right.

"The wedding should be last," grumbled the Sheikh as he looked at his wonderfully curvy wife, who was already showing from the new pregnancy even as she breast-fed their enormous, healthy son, the heir and future Sheikh of the island kingdom of Mizra.

"No," said Grace, tossing the schedule aside and looking down at her son, who was peacefully suckling away, eyes closed, oblivious to the drama and madness, the heartache and pain, the love and the loss from which he had emerged, fresh and innocent, screaming for air, howling for Mommy. "The baby shower is the most important event to me, and so I want that to end the evening."

"What about the wedding night! What kind of a woman does not want her wedding night! Ya Allah, do you not want your fairytale wedding? We will dance into the night, and—"

"I've already got my fairytale, Dhom," Grace whispered, her eyes tearing up as she touched her son's hair with one hand, her pregnant belly with the other. "And it took so much from so many people to get us here. I want to respect that. I want to cherish that."

"You do respect it, my love. And you do cherish it. There is no greater way to show it, Gracie," Dhom said, going to her and pulling her into a careful embrace, placing his own large hand on her belly.

"This isn't for show, and it isn't for symbolism. It's because I *want* to do it. It's because I *desperately* want to do it! You know that, don't you?" Grace said.

"Of course. Why else would I let those quack doctors even come near you?" Dhom said, frowning and trying to joke away the emotion that was making his voice waver.

"Clearly they aren't quacks. There was one egg of Zareena's left, and they were able to successfully fertilize it with your seed and then implant it in my womb. And my body accepted it, thank God!"

"How could there be any doubt your body would accept it?" Dhom said, kissing her on the cheek as he looked down at her belly again. "Ya Allah, I still cannot . . . cannot . . . ah, Zareena. You will live forever with us through your child. Do you see? Can you see? Can you hear?"

Of course I can, came the whisper on the afternoon breeze that swirled through the room, rustling the curtains, curling through their hair, tickling little Baby Dhom, caressing the husband, embracing the wife, the son, the daughter-to-come, and the mother.

Of course I can, came that whisper from the newest mother, who was now cradled in the universe's eternal womb. Of course I can.

∞

EPILOGUE
GUANTANOMO BAY HOLDING AREA

John Benson, head of the CIA's Dubai Field Office, blinked in the overhead light of the interrogation room as the blind old Sheikh of Kalyan drooled and pointed.

"A little to your left, old man," offered Benson.

"I am not pointing at you," said the Sheikh. "I am pointing at those creatures laughing at me."

Benson frowned and looked around the empty room. Then he shook his head as if to clear it, rubbing his eyes and leaning back in his metal chair. "OK, great. Now what is it, Kalyan? I am told you have been mumbling my name for months now, and since I was visiting the area to catch up with some old . . . friends, I thought I'd see what you've got for me."

"What I have for you? I have nothing! I have *done* nothing!" the old man wailed.

Benson sighed, rapping on the metal table. "You attempted to kill a United States citizen in a jurisdiction where U.S. law does not apply. That means terrorism, buddy. And that means Gitmo. No trial. No pleas. Nothing but three squares a day and a goddamn prayer mat. Got it?"

"It is not right!" shouted the old Sheikh. "I was barely in this story at all! And I am the one—"

"I hear ya, buddy," Benson muttered as he stood to leave. "We all want our own goddamn story. But these ain't our stories. And we ain't the storyteller."

"Then whose stories are they? And who is the goddamn storyteller?" the blind old Sheikh howled as Benson walked away.

There is only one storyteller, Benson thought as he lit a cigarette under an unusually large crescent moon that seemed to be smiling down from the Cuban sky. Because there is just one story, and it is all our stories.

The story of East and West.

The story of good and evil.

The story of man and woman.
The story of mother and child.
The story of love.

∞

From Annabelle Winters

Thanks for reading.

Join my private list at **annabellewinters.com/join** to get steamy epilogues, exclusive scenes with side characters, and a chance to join my advance review team.

And do write to me at **mail@annabellewinters.com** anytime. I really like hearing from you.

Love,
Anna.

Made in the USA
Columbia, SC
20 May 2022